"Thank you for keeping my kids safe, Christina."

Brett decided to take a chance, and wrapped an arm around her shoulders to squeeze her closer. Growing up, she'd always smelled of hair spray and drugstore perfume. Tonight Christina might as well have sprayed a perfume named Home.

Christina blinked. "Wow. I didn't think you could surprise me, but tonight, with those words, you've done it."

Because he'd been so rigid.

She was right. Something was changing inside him, probably thanks to an unrelenting pressure. If she knew that two urges were battling for control inside him, she'd be shocked. He was either going to kiss her or run for cover. There, in the warm glow of home, feeling connected, it seemed like the most natural thing in the world to press his lips to hers. What would she do?

Dear Reader,

Saving the Single Dad started while I was eavesdropping at work. (Note: beware the quiet writer.) A man stepped out of a meeting to take a call from his son. The reason? His son needed help negotiating some kind of agreement with his very clever sister. It was charming, but when Dad ended the call with a sweet "I love you, son," I was hooked. All I had to do was dream up the right heroine.

In *Saving the Single Dad*, Christina and Brett both have sharp edges, but such soft spots for kids and family that it was easy to help them fall in love. I hope you enjoy their story.

To find out more about my books and what's coming next, please visit me at cherylharperbooks.com.

Cheryl

HEARTWARMING

Saving the Single Dad

—

Cheryl Harper

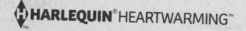
HARLEQUIN® HEARTWARMING™

ISBN-13: 978-1-335-63367-5

Saving the Single Dad

Printed in U.S.A.

Cheryl Harper discovered her love for books and words as a little girl, thanks to a mother who made countless library trips and an introduction to Laura Ingalls Wilder's Little House stories. Whether stories she reads are set in the prairie, the American West, Regency England or Earth a hundred years in the future, Cheryl enjoys strong characters who make her laugh. Now Cheryl spends her days searching for the right words while she stares out the window and her dog, Jack, snoozes beside her. And she considers herself very lucky to do so.

For more information about Cheryl's books, visit her online at cherylharperbooks.com or follow her on Twitter, @cherylharperbks.

Books by Cheryl Harper

Harlequin Heartwarming

Otter Lake Ranger Station

Smoky Mountain Sweethearts

Lucky Numbers

A Home Come True
Keeping Cole's Promise
Heart's Refuge
Winner Takes All

The Bluebird Bet
A Minute on the Lips

Visit the Author Profile page
at Harlequin.com for more titles.

CHAPTER ONE

CHRISTINA BRASWELL HAD already had enough of Monday, but it was only eight o'clock and the breakfast rush was in full swing. Finding her inner peace in the chatter and bustle that filled the combination camp store, marina and no-frills diner at the Otter Lake Campground was impossible.

Her inner peace had always been elusive like that. She focused on the view through the window. Otter Lake gleamed outside. The campground was situated in a quiet cove of the lake, a shadowy forest and the steep rise of Yanu Falls forming a serene landscape.

Which was almost the perfect contrast for the controlled chaos of the busy diner.

"I missed my favorite waitress this weekend," Woody Butler said as he yanked up his camo ball cap and smoothed down a healthy shock of white hair.

"Your wife steal the keys to the truck again?" Christina flipped over the porcelain coffee cup and poured black coffee to the rim. She was *his* favorite; Woody would swill coffee for hours and talk her ear off along the way before always leaving the same five-dollar tip.

Typical day ending in *Y* around here.

If he'd ever caught any of the fish he liked to tell her about, he'd done it before she started working behind the counter.

"Naw, you know better'n that, Chrissy," he said with a grin. "That wife of mine don't care what I do, so long's I stay out of her hair." He waggled his eyebrows. "That's why I like to hang out here with you."

Right. Christina had often wondered what lucky lady had married Woody right after Noah unloaded the ark, but they had discovered the key to long-term marital bliss: lots and lots of space.

Woody spent most of his hours telling waitresses fish stories. All in all, his hobby was harmless.

"You want the usual?" she asked out of habit. The menu was limited here, but the food was good enough to appease the tourists staying at the campground and enough locals from Sweetwater to keep a steady crowd coming through the place.

"Well, now...lemme see." Woody squinted at the two pages of menu and Christina tilted her head back and rolled her shoulders. Someday she would snap. The menu never changed. He had it memorized. Just about every person through the doors had been here often enough to recite the thing from memory, and still, this "lemme see" moment. There was no doubt in her mind that she was half a step above the world's worst morning-shift waitress, but now that her best friend had left town and taken Christina's car with her, this job was critical.

"I'll have me the pancakes with two eggs, over easy, and crispy bacon." Woody slapped the plastic-covered menu down as if he couldn't be prouder of himself for making that difficult decision. "You make sure Monroe gets the bacon crispy now." He pointed a finger. "I'd hate to leave a bad tip."

"Yes, Christina, I'll have the usual.

Thank you for asking." How hard was that to say?

Christina snatched up the menu, plopped it down on the leaning stack at the end of the counter and stuck her head in the window. "Short stack, two over easy, burn the bacon." The kid manning the griddle waved his spatula. Monroe didn't say much, but around here, Christina considered it a blessing. Until the rush started, she, Monroe and Luisa barely spoke. Every morning they enjoyed the warm glow of sunrise spreading across the lake. It was the only real perk of the job.

And of all the jobs she'd had, the Otter Lake Campground was her favorite, even with the annoyance and noise customers brought.

"You sure are looking nice today. Real…" Woody paused as he stared up at the ceiling, searching for the right word. Whatever adjective he picked, it was bound to be a doozy. "Swimsuit model–like."

Christina rubbed the center of her forehead in the effort to soothe the throb that had kicked up. If she thought about what that meant for too long, the throb would spread. He was proud of it and never meant to hurt her, but why couldn't she ever inspire "first grade teacher–like" or even "girl next door."

Then she would have blended easily with the good citizens of Sweetwater, Tennessee, something she'd never managed to do.

No one had ever disagreed she was pretty; few had ever called her nice.

When her cell phone rang, Christina pulled it out of her tight jeans pocket and checked the caller ID.

Her best friend. She didn't want to talk to Leanne. She wanted to *shout* at Leanne.

Woody leaned forward as if he could read the number across the counter, but Christina turned away and answered the call.

"I'm at work. I can't talk." Christina walked down to the quietest corner, where she could see the boats lined up at the dock. Most of the early-morning mist had burned off already. The weather forecast was for a beautiful, warm day.

"If you'd answered any of my other calls, we might have had some time to talk when it was convenient," Leanne snapped. Christina immediately straightened.

"Are you okay?" she asked, and covered her ear with one hand. There was something about the tremor in Leanne's voice that reminded her of the bad times. It had been almost ten years since her best friend had dumped her drug problem, but that tremor had scared Christina enough that she'd never forget it.

"Fine. Just missing my kids." Leanne laughed breathlessly. "And no one in your crummy town will answer their phones."

"*My* crummy town?" They'd grown up here together, two poor girls with busted families in a trailer park at the dead end of a dusty gravel road. For a long time, they'd been tighter than sisters. Christina listened as Leanne took a drag on something. She hoped it was a cigarette.

"Brett? Have you been calling Brett?" Christina tightened her grip on her phone until her hand ached. Thanks to this ill-conceived disappearing act, Leanne's ex-husband, Brett, had run out of patience with her. If Leanne pushed this, ignored his latest demand that her only contact with their kids be in person and only when he was around, Brett might eliminate all her visitation rights. What was she thinking? "You know that's a bad idea. Give him space. He'll come around."

"I called Brett. His mama. Every friend I thought I had left in Sweetwater, but you're the only one to answer, girl. I knew I could depend on you." Leanne's change of tone was the first clue about the reason she'd phoned.

Whenever Leanne started to butter her up, the thing that came next was going to be upsetting.

"How's my car?" Christina asked in a desperate attempt to head off whatever request Leanne had. "And Beau? I guess he's okay, too." Whatever Beau had been, it hadn't been a good boyfriend, but if Leanne felt guilty, maybe she'd figure out her problem on her own.

"Your rust bucket is still rolling and I'll bring it back as soon as I can." Leanne cleared her throat. "But I need you to do something for me first."

Still no mention of the man Christina had dated three times, only because she couldn't be bothered to tell him she had to shampoo her hair. Beau was in Sweetwater temporarily to work at the Smoky Valley Nature Reserve, home of Otter Lake. The fact that she couldn't say what he did for a living suggested neither one of them had been serious about their relationship. Beau and Leanne might not even be together anymore. Maybe he'd gone home and forgotten to tell her about it.

"Well, all this walking I'm having to do to get to work and back has seriously hampered my free time." Christina hoped the words were convincing. Leanne and her kids were all the family Christina had left, so she'd do whatever Leanne asked if it was possible. Forever.

Always had. Always would.

It had been months since she'd seen Leanne's kids, even from a distance, but Brett Hendrix was doing his best to keep them in sight at all times. While he was no grand find as a compassionate, forgiving human being, he was a good father. Strong. He'd keep his kids safe, and no matter how much she missed Riley and Parker, Christina wouldn't fault their father for doing what he felt he had to do for their well-being.

Hearing one too many stories about Leanne coming out of Sweetwater's one and only bar had been his final straw. Christina had immediately waded in to defend Leanne, who'd only been keeping her company as she closed up, because Leanne had already been exiled. She'd had nothing to lose. Brett didn't trust either one of them to tell him the truth and a court battle had settled the issue. He had sole custody of the kids and he wielded it like a weapon.

Whatever part she'd played in the blowup might keep her awake at night, but if this had been the moment to chase Leanne back to the pills that had taken over her life, Christina would never forgive Brett Hendrix.

"Come home, Leanne. Nothing will change with Brett if you don't." Fatigue was a nearly constant battle Christina fought, but it settled heavily over her. She knew Leanne was going to refuse.

"I said I'm bringing your car back. A couple weeks, that's all I need," Leanne shouted. Christina yanked the phone away from her ear and tried not to concentrate on how short Leanne's temper had gotten the first time she'd fallen down the drug rabbit hole. This was emotion running high. Leanne would never be stupid enough to try drugs again.

When Monroe slid Woody's plate into the window, Christina knew her time had run out. "What do you want?"

"Send me a picture of the kids. Please. I miss them. And if you have a chance to talk to Brett, convince him to reconsider letting me talk to them. One phone call. Please." Leanne's voice shook at the last.

"Come home, Leanne. The only way to fix this is if you come home." Christina smiled at Woody to stall his impatient gestures for his food cooling in the window.

"I can't. Not right now. Things aren't good." Leanne sniffed loudly and Christina fought the shiver that crept down her spine. "I'll be home soon, though."

"Where are you?" Christina asked. "I'll come get you." She had no idea how she'd get there, but she'd steal the keys to Woody's truck herself if it meant saving Leanne from whatever was going on.

"Not now. See if you can talk to Riley and Parker. After school?" Leanne asked. "You could drop by, pick them up and take them to McDonald's. Parker still loves the playground there." Leanne took another drag.

"Pick them up? In my arms? Because I have no *car*." Christina shook her head. "Just get back here, Leanne. We'll go to McDonald's together. Until then, I can't help you."

She ended the call over her friend's protests, marched to the window to pick up Woody's plate, took a deep breath, and then turned to slide it in front of him. "Sorry about that. A small emergency." When she realized her hands were shaking, Christina made tight fists.

Would telling Leanne no ever get easier?

Woody's puckered mouth didn't ease until she flashed him the smile she'd used ever since she was seven years old and realized a bit of innocence could get her out of a scrape. "I hope you aren't too mad."

His long sigh as he unwrapped his silverware faded as she leaned one elbow on the counter next to him. "What can I do to make it up to you?" If he complained to the manager, it would be her second in a week. Since she'd been late two mornings in a row, thanks to the complete lack of friendlies who'd pick up a hitchhiker, Christina had to do whatever she could to soothe his ruffled,feathers. Luisa was a great boss, but she wouldn't forget unhappy customers easily.

Woody tapped his half-empty coffee cup. "Fill 'er up. Keep me company. That's all, sweetness." He'd always be easy to jolly out of a bad mood. Woody was a sucker for a friendly smile.

Christina tipped the pot up and watched the other tables in her section. "Where you headed out today?" Christina asked.

"Thought I might troll over closer to the falls." Woody slurped his coffee. "Should be nice and cool."

Christina nodded and propped the other elbow on the counter. Stretching the muscles in her back felt good.

"You could come with me." He waggled his eyebrows as he shoved a forkful of egg in his mouth, one drop of yolk landing on his chin. While he chewed, he said, "Be happy to save you the long walk home."

Christina offered him his own paper napkin. People who waited tables should not be as completely grossed out by dribbles as she was, but it couldn't be helped.

"Were you eavesdropping on my phone call, Woody? Naughty." She ignored the lurch of worry in her stomach at the reminder of Leanne's request.

He took a bite of his pancakes and completely ignored the stray syrup that landed on his chin. "Heard about it in town first. Leanne stole your car, huh? And your man. Friends like that, you don't need enemies, am I right?" He didn't seem all that worried about the serious downturn in her luck.

She'd learned to expect that same attitude from most of Sweetwater, so it didn't surprise her. Charity at Christmastime? The town could pull together for that, but everyday caring for people with real trouble was less common. She'd find the solution to her problems on her own, like she had her whole life.

Being flat broke, stuck in a town that

hated her and in serious need of a way out was nothing new.

She'd also take care of Leanne. Always had. Always would.

"Guess everyone's talking about Leanne," Christina said as she replayed Leanne's phone call in her head. In the same spot, Christina might not be in a big rush to come home, either.

Except she couldn't imagine walking out on her kids. Ever.

"She pops up now and again. Things died down after the de-vorce," Woody said, hitting the first syllable hard. "Then she disappeared with Beau, and you and her are both topics of convos regular-like."

"Leanne and Beau aren't together. It's a coincidence they left town at the same time." Christina had no idea if it were true, but Woody could start that rumor circulating and get them some benefit of the doubt.

And it wasn't the first occasion she'd lied to make the people of Sweetwater let go of a juicy tidbit.

She and Leanne ought to be used to being the subject of speculation. For their whole lives, they'd been the town's guilty pleasure. They'd grown up in the same place where people with no other options landed. Christina's father had been in jail, so her mother worked two jobs to pay the bills, leaving Christina in charge, and Leanne's grandmother finished raising all but one of her absent son's kids. Climbing on the big school bus of staring children had been easier with Leanne at her back. Being on the outside never got better, but at least they had each other. And all those good people gossiping in town? Sure, someone ought to do something to help Christina and Leanne, but it was more fun to talk about them behind their backs.

"Brett and them kids are eating out in town ever' day," Woody added, "getting lots of sympathy, you know?" Of course he was. Brett was the hero in the story.

That was another constant. Brett Hendrix was a good man, day in and out, without fail.

He also handed down pronouncements like a heavenly judge on high.

At seventeen, Leanne had done the smartest thing she could: gotten pregnant by the class president. Instead of pretending he didn't know Leanne or weaseling his way out of any responsibility, Brett had proposed.

Marrying Brett had straightened Leanne out and Christina was able to finish high school and even two years at a community college. Things were okay, except Brett never wanted Christina around. At least Leanne had ignored his orders.

Until Leanne messed it all up. Drugs had nearly destroyed them all, but Brett had pulled Leanne out. For that reason, Christina would always consider herself a Brett Hendrix fan.

Even when he made her so mad she wanted to throw darts at a lifelike depiction of his handsome face.

Which was all the time lately.

"I better check my other tables, Woody," Christina said, the sadness that rolled over her when she wondered what was going to happen to Leanne hard to ignore. Space would make it easier to build her shell again.

"Just come back to me. We can talk about your transportation. Be happy to give you a ride wherever. Retirement's a true blessing, open schedule for days, don't ya know." Woody snapped a piece of charred bacon and chewed.

Christina picked up her order pad and her coffeepot. She moved between the tables, refilling and dropping checks off at tables as she went. There was usually a question about the easiest way to get back to Gatlinburg or where the fish were biting. Directions were easy. There weren't many choices.

And she always gave the same answer about the fish. It didn't matter. Fish were notorious for making liars out of people.

She approached the last table in the corner. "Can I get you anything else?" she asked as she slipped a ticket under the cup she was filling.

"How about your phone number?" the bearded guy asked. She didn't recognize him, but that was normal. People came and went all the time because of the campground. If she had a dollar for every time some guy on his yearly fishing trip hit on her, she might be able to swing another car.

"Sorry. I'm seeing someone." She gave him a friendly smile and stepped away from the table. When she was younger, she'd fallen for enough charming out-of-towners to learn what a waste of time it was to look for Prince Charming in a man passing through town. Now she went straight for a lie, the easiest brush-off of all.

"Sure have been friendly to the old guy at the counter. Flirting for tips?" he asked. The complete lack of a smile on his face made her a bit nervous.

"No, just an old friend." Christina tightened her grip on the coffeepot. She'd left bartending for this reason. Give a man alcohol and he was convinced he was the World's Sexiest Man capable of taking what he wanted at the same time.

Removing alcohol had made confrontations like this a lot less common.

That didn't mean she'd forgotten how to make a weapon out of whatever was at hand, though.

"I'd like to be a new friend," he said as he leaned forward. "Besides, heard him say something about somebody stealing your boyfriend. Now, if you can give me her number, I'll go away. Any woman who could take a man from a looker like you must be the stuff of legends." He grabbed her wrist as Christina moved to leave.

No matter how she turned her hand, she couldn't twist free. Setting down the coffeepot to claw at his fingers would leave her with nothing but her pencil as a weapon.

Determined not to cause a brawl at this job, Christina said, "While I do appreciate the kindness, sir, I've got to get back to work." *And if I shove my pencil in your eye, I will probably lose this job.*

"Feisty." The guy tilted his head to the side. "Woman like you, dressed like that. Can't imagine you ain't in the market for something." There was no doubt in Christina's mind that her hot-pink shirt and tight jeans were gone in his mind.

Before she could swing the coffeepot or make a stab with her pencil, Woody eased off his stool, hitched up his belt and said, "You need help, Chrissy?"

The last thing she needed was for Woody to wade into this mess. She didn't want his injuries on her conscience, and she couldn't afford a bill for repairs.

Christina moved to set the coffeepot

down on the guy's arm and jerked away
as soon as he let go of her arm.

"Oh my. I almost got you." She shook her
head as if she couldn't believe how clumsy
she was. "I do apologize." Should she offer
to cover his breakfast in order to get him
out of there?

What would she do if he returned when
the crowd thinned?

Call the cops before his backside hit the
wooden seat, that's what. Being nice as a
solution didn't get more than one shot.

When the guy stood up, she and Woody
both shrank back a step. He was big. Of
course he was. What rule of nature made
it necessary for the biggest animal on the
food chain to be the one with the fewest
redeeming qualities?

Armed with her coffeepot in one hand
and her pencil in the other, Christina
squared off. "You go ahead and leave, mis-
ter. I've got your ticket covered."

She would much rather lose the ten dollars than the job. And if the guy did come
back, she'd gladly shut him down and kiss
the diner goodbye. In the meantime, she
was no one's victim. Not anymore.

Before the guy could make up his mind whether to throw his weight around some more or skip out on his bill and count himself lucky, the door to the restaurant opened and the park's head law enforcement ranger, Brett Hendrix, stepped in.

The relief that swept over her was immediate, yet enraging. He had the same golden glow he'd had as he sauntered the halls of Sweetwater High, everyone's friend and role model. Why couldn't he have gained forty pounds and lost all but forty strands of hair? Probably wouldn't matter. He inspired trust and that would always be attractive.

They must have appeared as if frozen, caught in the instant before chairs started flying, punches were thrown and someone howled in pain, because Brett braced both hands on his belt, his gun holstered but within easy reach, and said, "Oh good. I made it in time for the brawl. I hate to miss the first minute because then I can never follow the rest of the story."

Christina didn't exactly relax, because Leanne's ex was no fan of hers, but he knew right from wrong and never wavered from it.

Brett Hendrix believed there was no gray area when it came to life's challenges, only seeing things as either totally black or white. It made life hard for those living in mostly those gray areas, especially for Christina. She knew he was a loving father, but she wanted to help her friend, too.

It was easy to hate him for all that, but right now, watching her would-be stalker fold before her eyes, Brett's presence warmed a tiny corner of her cold heart.

Even better, faced with a park ranger in his officially official flat hat and everything, the guy yanked a twenty from his wallet, dropped the money on the table and stomped out.

Not only did she not have to cover his tab, but he'd left her the best tip of the day.

Christina couldn't help the grin that slowly turned up her lips as she shoved her pencil back in her ponytail. "My hero."

She waved the twenty-dollar bill and check at Woody. "You, too, darling." His thin chest puffed out as if he'd done something besides stand behind her and bluster, but that was okay. Any thoughts of complaining about his cold breakfast and indifferent service were gone.

"What can I get you, Ranger?" Christina asked as she sashayed back behind the counter. She tried to always sashay when Brett was around. It made his scowl darker.

"First, tell me what that was." He stared hard at the door.

"You know, one more guy who wants to hassle me," Christina replied as she noticed Woody glued to the conversation. "New guy, so there was some excitement. All the others have learned where the boundary is." She smiled at Brett.

"Business as usual, then," Brett said with a nod. "Two coffees, two slices of pecan pie, to go."

Christina saluted and turned to box up his order, happy to have her routine restored to calm the jitters.

The weight of Brett's disapproving stare rattled her again, but it was familiar at least. When his phone rang and he turned away to answer it, Christina managed to catch her breath. As soon as Brett was on his way, she might even take Woody up on his offer of a ride home.

And if that didn't illustrate how bad things were, that Christina Braswell was about to ask for help, she'd eat the pencil she'd been prepared to wield like a spear.

CHAPTER TWO

OBVIOUSLY THIS WAS going to be the Mondayest Monday of all Mondays. Brett had started the morning with a disaster before moving directly into a showdown and followed that up with a yelling match.

All before leaving the house.

In about two minutes, he'd be late for the meeting his boss, Ash Kingfisher, had called. Since he was at least ten minutes away from the ranger station at this point, he needed to come up with a logical excuse.

Any nature reserve staff who'd observed his drive in had probably already called to report him for reckless driving. The rolling stop he'd made at the first four-way off the highway had not been his proudest moment.

And now, instead of hustling to get his order, Christina Braswell was doing some kind of deep breathing exercises, her eyes closed, and his son was on the phone.

Since he'd just dropped the kid off at school, after calmly mopping up spilled grape juice that was all Parker would drink with his microwaved waffles, followed by changing his uniform, he wasn't keen on catching up.

Then he realized Parker was his best source to tracking Riley, his daughter who was thirteen-going-on-thirty, and he answered, "What's up, buddy?"

"Dad, Riley said she'll give me ten dollars if I do her chores when we get home this afternoon. That's a good deal, right?" Parker said, and gasped as if he was running down the hall. They'd been on time when he dropped them off, but Parker's curiosity led him astray. A lot.

First grade was all about exciting new things.

"We've talked about this. Riley doesn't have your best interests at heart, son. Remember that and try to think about her offers with that in mind." Brett glanced over his shoulder to see that Christina had managed to shake loose of her meditation to bag up his order. She'd put two cups right next to the bag. He should have kept an eye on her. A wise man never turned his back on an angry woman.

Interrupting whatever little showdown she'd been caught in the middle of might be the first thing that had worked for him that morning. He hoped it wasn't the last. She'd never thank him. She never had been the grateful sort, not even when he'd done his best to make sure she was safe. For a split second, he'd wanted to try that all over again, but the woman had more sharp edges than shattered glass.

"But it's folding clothes, Dad. And she said she'd help me with my room." Parker sneezed and Brett could almost hear the nurse's phone call telling him his son needed to come home. Right now, no fever meant no sick day.

"What happened the last time she made that offer?" he asked as he pulled his wallet out. With one raised eyebrow, he asked Christina his total. She took a ten from him and turned to the cash register.

"She tricked me." Parker's sad voice made Brett smile. Having a daughter with an impressive criminal mind was scary. He'd only managed to stop her from shaving off her hair because Parker had asked him where his clippers were that morning. He'd had to learn to follow the trail to anticipate however Riley would act up next, and it often started with his trusting son.

Since her mother had gone off the deep end again, Riley needed careful attention. How to help her eluded him, but keeping her safe wouldn't.

"Right. Don't let her trick you again. This morning she almost got you, so watch her, P." Brett took his change and shoved it in his pocket. "Now, be good. Pay attention. Call me when you get home this afternoon."

"I will, Dad." Parker heaved a huge sigh. "Girls are tricky."

"Don't you ever forget it, son." With his wife's best friend watching his every move, he couldn't argue with that. "I love you, Parker."

"Love you—" The call ended before he finished the rest of the sentence. That was Parker's usual goodbye, so it was more reassuring than worrying.

When he ended the call, he considered calling Riley to explain again how much he disliked her attempts at tricking her brother. Then he remembered her annoyed stare when he'd steered her out of the bathroom and away from the statement she wanted to make with her hair.

Dinnertime would be soon enough to tackle that.

And since he was headed to Nashville for a weeklong training session, it might be dinner *next* week.

Looking forward to a class on managing a law enforcement department like it was a trip to Hawaii was a sign of how out of control his house had gotten. There would be no grape juice, no sullen teenage stares, and if he wanted to watch something other than the cartoon channel, he could. The business class hotel he'd booked on the outskirts of Nashville sounded more and more like heaven.

"Long day," Christina drawled as she pushed the cups toward him.

"Yeah. And it's just started." He shook his head as she slid the sugar packets over. Then he ripped both open and dumped them in the coffee. He wadded up the paper and Christina slipped the lid on.

"How are Parker and Riley?" she asked as she tipped her chin up. She expected him to tell her to go jump in Otter Lake and he wanted to. Anything he said to her would go right back to Leanne. He didn't have the energy for a confrontation.

"They're okay." Brett snatched up the bag and pointed at the empty table in the corner. "He going to be a problem?"

Christina twirled her pen as she considered his question. Even in the fluorescent lights of the campground's dumpy restaurant, she was a heartbreaker. For a split second after he'd married her best friend, he'd tried to act the big brother and protect her. At seventeen, she'd run circles around him immediately and basically made him wish he'd never been born. More than a decade later, he could see the hardness in her eyes and wished he'd done a better job.

"I had it under control." She shrugged a shoulder. "Woody had my back." Out of the corner of his eye, Brett saw the old guy straighten on his stool.

Pretending to have everything under control was his move, so he respected it.

The glint in her eye was a warning, and

it was always there. She'd never wanted his help, and she wouldn't take him up on it if he offered to handle her problem customer for her.

If he wasn't careful, his daughter would have the same calculating expression.

"You've got my number if he comes back," Brett said as he dug around in his pocket for a dollar bill. He was ticked off at Leanne, and Christina was guilty by association, but he couldn't walk out without leaving a tip or at least making the offer.

"I won't call it." She pointed at Woody Butler, frequent camp fly at the Otter Lake Campground. "I've got Woody."

Since the last time Woody might have been able to throw a punch was forty years ago, Brett was almost certain he'd be a hindrance if it came to a real fight.

Now he was fifteen minutes late for that meeting with his boss, and he shouldn't be wasting his time trying to tell her to do the right thing anyway.

He held up the bag and headed for the door.

"Hey, Brett," Christina called.

He could pretend he didn't hear her, like

his mother had when he'd yelled at her to get out of bed before he left that morning. Diane Hendrix had come for a visit three years ago to help him out, and every day since, her patience grew shorter. Their yelling match over the imposition of him disappearing for a week and leaving everything on her shoulders had been the cherry on top of his Dumpster sundae.

But he was in uniform, so he did the right thing. "Yeah?"

"You're probably wondering how Leanne is. Your wife." Christina crossed her arms over her chest. "The wife you cut out of her kids' lives."

"Ex-wife. For good reasons, which most of the people in this room are very aware of," Brett muttered as he glanced around the restaurant. The crowd had thinned, but he could see a few regulars. Anybody who knocked around Otter Lake or Sweetwater had heard their story already. Cheating, drugs and the epic court battle made for juicy gossip. His reputation would never recover, but he wanted better for Riley and Parker.

"She misses her kids." Christina stepped closer.

"She should have thought of that a long time ago." Brett bit back the rest of the answer that bubbled up.

"She wasn't drinking at the Branch, Brett." Christina glanced over her shoulder and he could see the frustration on her face when she turned back. She didn't want this to play out in public, either. "You told her not to talk to me, but we're best friends. She came to keep me company. That's it. Cutting her out like this, have you thought what it might mean? What it means to Parker and Riley to lose their mother, or to Leanne to lose the most important things in her life, the kids who keep her grounded?"

Christina clenched her hands together in the apron tied around her waist. Instead of impassive control, her expression was a mix of begging and warning. He understood her message, too, but there was nothing he could do about it. He'd made his decision about what to do about Leanne the day the judge gave him sole custody. While she was in Sweetwater, he'd invited her over to visit the kids but only when he was around. What had been exciting and passionate when they were kids had become unstable and a problem when they'd become parents. He'd wanted his children to know their mother, but she'd left them behind.

Now that she'd gone? She was out of all of their lives for good.

That meant everything was on his plate. No matter how much the load weighed him down, he had to keep everything balanced.

Leanne had thrown away her chance to prove she was ready for more responsibility. He refused to admit any guilt, but his whole world was fraying around the edges.

"I don't know what to tell you, Chris." The old nickname slipped out and he watched her shoulders slump. "You know my priority." He backed out of the door and watched her turn away. He was going to escape the town's scrutiny; Christina would have to face it, this time alone.

She'd made her choice. He understood her loyalty, but that loyalty had made it easy enough for Leanne to make bad decisions. He was doing the right thing.

Once he was back in the car, he called

the latest in a string of women he'd dated in an attempt to find another wife. If he didn't have permanent help and soon with the kids, he'd have to give up his job.

He'd had a strict list of requirements for the women he dated, since the only thing he never wanted to have happen again was to be lied to and abandoned. This teacher from Knoxville was prettier than he preferred, but she was quiet and sweet and so boring that he couldn't imagine her being the subject of the kind of wild stories that circulated about Leanne or Christina.

She also hadn't grown up in Sweetwater. At this point, that was her strongest selling point. Living with people who'd witnessed his biggest failure from the front row was hard enough. He didn't want his children facing that memory at home every day.

He was planning to leave a message, but Lila answered. "Hello?"

"Hey, I figured you'd be teaching," Brett said as he maneuvered the curvy road that led to the ranger station and the overlook.

"Free period," Lila said before clearing her throat. "But I'm glad you called."

"Well, I wanted to remind you that I'll be

in Nashville this week." Brett studied the parking lots as he passed. Low occupancy currently, but the numbers would grow later in the day. "When I get back, I'd like you to come out and meet my kids." He'd decided their conversations had gone well enough that it was time to move to the next step. After four false starts, he had a good feeling about Lila. He'd show his mother he was making progress, so that he could talk her into staying until school was out for the year. That was going to be stretching his persuasive abilities, but he didn't think Lila would want to marry in the middle of the school year.

"About that." Lila cleared her throat delicately. "I don't think that's a good plan."

Brett pulled into his parking spot and turned off the engine. "Why not? I'd love to do it sooner, but—"

"I'm seeing someone else, Brett. You and me, the two of us together don't work. We have no spark." Lila sighed. "I'm not telling you anything you don't know. What I don't understand is why you seem to think it's still a good thing."

Brett thumped his head on the steering wheel and closed his eyes. Hysterical laughter was going to be the next step, but he'd fight it as long as he could.

"Are you still there?" she asked softly.

"Yep. No spark, huh?" He'd never tried to stir up a spark. He and Leanne had been nothing but sparks, down to fiery explosions. He didn't want that anymore.

He wanted someone nurturing for his kids, someone who wouldn't flake when a better offer came along or desert him when Riley pulled whatever stunt she was planning next.

And he wanted peace.

What was he going to do?

"Okay, well…" Brett picked up the bribe, the critical bag of pie from the diner. "Glad I made the call."

"You're a great guy. I know you'll find the woman you deserve," Lila said before she ended the call.

When he had a minute, he'd come up with a new plan. Right now, he had to go and make sure his boss didn't fire him.

As he strode past the front desk, Macy Gentry, the woman who kept the ranger station operational while treating guests like VIPs, whistled. "He's called twice looking for you."

No doubt. Ash Kingfisher had a million different balls in the air as the supervisor for this ranger station. He didn't need to be kept waiting.

Brett tapped on the boss's door, and then entered, waving the white bag as a flag of surrender. "I brought pie."

Ash grunted, and then pointed at the ratty seat across from him. "Thought cops were supposed to be about doughnuts." They had this conversation at least once a week. Brett had started out as a cop in Knoxville. As a kid, he'd wanted nothing more than to get out of Sweetwater and the shadow of the nature reserve. As soon as Leanne had told him about their second baby on the way, he'd decided Sweetwater might be the only place that could save them.

In Knoxville, Leanne could get into too much trouble. In Sweetwater, any trouble she found would eventually make its way back to him. Unfortunately, that made it harder to love her.

"Doughnuts, pie, mainly pastries in general. We try not to discriminate." Brett slid the second cup of coffee over and watched Ash tug the lid off and drink deep. He must have already had a full Monday, too.

"You all set for this management class?" Ash asked as he shuffled papers across his desk.

Brett grumbled. That was the best answer he could come up with. He'd been a ranger at the Smoky Valley Nature Reserve for more than five years. This promotion to senior law enforcement officer was nice, but it came with headaches he hadn't anticipated. This step was required, though, so he'd get through it.

"Doesn't matter. I've postponed the training as long as I can. Go, or...else." Ash held out both hands. "Can't change the rules for you, right?"

Brett understood that. Arguing about his personal situation or explaining how well he was already performing would accomplish nothing. "No, sir."

"Before you go, I wanted to talk to you about this *opportunity* the chief ranger sent our way." Ash pulled out a file folder. "State's looking to set up regional law enforcement task forces focused on terrorist activities. I'm not sure how the nature reserve can be involved. I suspect the chief ranger is not certain, either. However, we both think you're the best man for the job." Ash leaned back in his chair and claimed one of the containers of pie.

Brett could understand their thinking. There was a good chance he'd worked with the other agencies involved in East Tennessee. After the day he'd had, all he wanted to do was put his head on the desk and rest. "I'd be happy to, sir. Whatever I can do for the reserve. You know that."

Ash sighed as he took a bite of the pie. "Well, I figured you'd say that, so I already put your name in. It means monthly meetings in Knoxville."

Brett finished off his coffee and wished for more. The pie was sweet, but only coffee would give him the kick he needed to go any further with this day.

"You look like a man who's running on fumes, Hendrix." Ash took another bite of pie. "Anything I need to know about?"

If Ash hadn't already heard about his

woes through the grapevine, Brett wouldn't be the man to tell him.

"Nope, I'm going to stop by the office, make sure the patrols are set. Macy has all my contact info and I'll have my cell." Brett picked up his hat and stood.

"Keep me posted and thank you for your service." Ash waved his empty container. "I learned that from a weeklong training session at the Tennessee Law Enforcement Officers Academy. See what an effective manager I became?"

"They do good work," Brett said with a reluctant smile.

"Yes, they do. Make sure you get some sleep. I can't have you napping in your car. Watch the speed limit on your way back down, and the stop signs here on the reserve mean full stops, not hesitations. Got it?"

Brett opened his mouth, but there was no answer to that, so he nodded.

"I see everything." Ash dumped the plastic container into a garbage can.

"Recycle," Macy yelled from her desk. Firmly.

"Eyes in the back of her head," Ash muttered before cursing and fishing out the container.

"If that's all you needed…" Brett stood next to the door, his hand on the knob as he plotted his next steps. He had to be in Nashville by three. He'd be cutting it close.

"Dismissed." Ash nodded, and then added, "Hey, Hendrix, I know things right now are rough. If it gets to be too much, tell me."

Brett agreed, and then stepped out. There was no way he'd ask his boss for help. That would be a sure path to the sidelines. He loved his job. He didn't want to sit out any of the action.

Not even a task force that amounted to lunches filled with gossip all in the name of cooperation.

After he had a chance to check in with the rangers on patrol and to double-check the schedule that he'd double-checked every day for the past two weeks, he slid back into his car and hit the road.

With every mile, the certainty that something would go wrong grew. He hated being away from his kids. In a last-ditch effort to calm his nerves, he phoned his mother.

"Did you call to apologize?" she said without any other hello.

"No, I called to thank you." No good would come of explaining how much more he needed her to do than she was already doing.

Her huff was the answer he'd expected. "And to warn you Riley's up to something. It involves her hair. She's either planning to cut it off or make me think that's what she's doing while she does something else." Brett tightened his hands on the steering wheel and wished her acting out would stop there. If it made her feel better, he'd hand her the clippers himself.

But nothing seemed to make her feel better. Her mother had left town. Riley was angry.

She deserved to be angry.

"Well, as long as she's not trying to hurt anybody else, I guess that's good enough." His mother never had been great at encouragement. Now the only thought that stuck in his brain was that Riley might go past teenage drama to something worse.

"Try to go easy on her. I'll call tonight to make sure the day went okay." Brett wondered if he should tell his mother Lila had bailed, too, or let the whole situation ride until he was home.

"Sounds fine," she said, "but I wanted to let you know I signed up for a singles cruise in December. Don't know how this thing with the new lady is going, but you could set up a visit around then. Lots of happy family time. Holidays. Cheer in the air, all that."

His mother had been desperate to get back to the life of the single retiree almost from the first week she'd arrived to help. He wasn't sure he blamed her because there wasn't much for her in Sweetwater, but the extra drop of bad news was more than he could take.

"All right. We'll figure it out. Talk to you tonight, Mom." He ended the call before she could squawk that her name was Diane and he should learn to use it.

That was how most arguments between them finished. He liked to tick her off by calling her Mom. To get that dig in without crossing whatever line he was unwilling to go over. She'd been the world's coolest mom growing up, mainly because he'd raised himself. Now, as a grandmother, she'd prefer to be all expensive gifts from faraway places and infrequent trips home.

The women in his life were questionable. Lila could have been the exception and she'd bailed before he'd even rowed the boat out from shore.

There was an important lesson in there.

He had no brainpower left to work it out. He had to get to Nashville to learn to manage people.

The joke, once he got it, was great. Managing the rangers who served with him was a piece of pecan pie. Sweet and easy as a to-go order. It was the people who lived in his house that he needed training for. He had a feeling that the Tennessee Law Enforcement Officers Academy had seen a whole lot worse than his family, but that didn't mean there was an instructor there prepared to teach him how to make order out of that chaos.

CHAPTER THREE

THE THING ABOUT being almost alone in the world was that the requests Leanne made led Christina to do things she would never otherwise do. It had taken a solid day to make up her mind, but Christina had finally given in. Lurking outside the Sweetwater school right after the last bell was so far from how she wanted to be spending her afternoon that it might as well have been some other person's life.

But Leanne had asked.

If word got back to Brett, he would be angry and it would confirm his suspicions, so she had to be careful.

Woody had given her a ride into town, dropping her off in front of city hall so that she could pay her taxes. She wasn't sure what taxes he thought were due, but Woody was the kind of friend who didn't look at things too closely. At this point, that made him the perfect friend. At his insistence that she might need a getaway driver, or bail money, she'd gone so far as to put his number in her phone. When her next morning shift rolled around, she owed him endless hot coffee, for sure.

The fact that he'd changed his plans to do her a favor without requiring anything in return warmed the dark corner of her heart. Woody was good people, no doubt. Were there more around if she looked for them?

"Hope all the other good people around here are very busy," Christina muttered as she did her best to pretend she belonged on the sidewalk next to the elementary school.

If she could talk to the kids and snap a picture before the bus pulled away, or some vigilant mother called the cops, this scheme would be one step up from a total disaster.

As soon as Riley stepped outside, she pulled her cell phone out of her backpack and started texting. Her heart-shaped face was so familiar and had changed so much since the last time Christina had seen her. What hadn't changed was the frown. Christina eased up next to her. "Texting your boyfriend?"

Instead of jumping in surprise, Riley turned ninety degrees in a classic display of the cold shoulder. Her dark hair lifted in the breeze, but that was the only movement. The rest of her was statue still and apparently in no mood for conversation.

While Christina was plotting the best scenario to keep her in place, Parker launched a surprise attack. "Aunt Chris, what are you doing here? Did you come to pick us up?" Parker's arms were wrapped so tightly around her middle that Christina had to ease him back to take a deep breath.

"Sorry, Parks, not today. I just wanted to say hi before you got on the bus." Christina studied his face. Other than the disappointment wrinkling his brow, Parker's sweet face was completely the same, so earnest. She could see faint traces of Leanne in his nose and chin, but the rest of him was all Brett. Serious brown eyes made it hard not to give him exactly what he wanted.

"Oh, since Dad's out of town?" Parker asked as he yanked hard on Riley's T-shirt. "Don't be so rude." That order made him sound like his father, too.

"No, because I've missed you. I talked to

your mother and she wanted to make sure I told you that she's headed back home to Sweetwater soon." Christina wasn't sure why she said it, but she wanted it to be true.

Riley was shaking her head as she looked up from her phone. "Don't buy it, Parker. She knows you're still a waste. Mom won't be back until you're out of the house. I'll have to wait until then to see her again. We talked about it on the phone."

"You got to talk to her?" Parker's lip trembled, but he didn't let a tear fall. Instead, he balled up a fist and punched his sister in the arm. "Shut up. Dad told me not to listen to a word you say."

"No, thanks to your beloved aunt, neither of us can talk to Mom." Riley snarled and rubbed the spot before marching away.

Christina wrapped her arm tightly around Parker's shoulders and leaned down to murmur, "Your dad gave you good advice, Parks. Older sisters, they like to torment their younger brothers. Ignore her right now. Eventually, they grow out of it." Leanne had always told her kids that "Aunt Chris" might as well have been her baby sister. Christina offered him her fist to bump. When he returned the bump, she blew up her hand before pressing kisses all over his cheeks. "Us young ones have to stick together."

"Sure thing, Aunt Chris. Just for that, she can do her own chores." Parker hitched up his backpack and looked over his shoulder at the bus waiting to take them home. Something had changed in his eyes, some of the joy was gone. Did he believe Riley was telling the truth about Leanne's distance being Christina's fault? What could she do about it if he did? "Unless you're giving us a ride, we better go. Diane gets mad if she has to come pick us up. Missing the bus leads to slamming doors, so..."

Diane? That was the weirdest thing about Brett's family. He was all Mr. America and everything, but his mother insisted her grandkids call her by her first name. She also dressed like a college freshman and had a gambling problem. How had he turned out so well?

"Aunt Chris won't be driving us anywhere, Parker," Riley drawled. "She's got no car. Everyone in town's talking about it." And her mother. Christina tried to catch

Riley's shoulder, but the girl was already trotting toward the bus. She presented a hard shell, but Christina had lived inside the same lie for too long not to recognize it.

Riley was too young to be having to put up with the gossip and disappointment of a messed-up family.

Since she'd never been able to fix similar problems for herself, Christina wasn't sure how to address it.

Parker's anxious frown was enough to convince Christina to let things go for one more day. She grabbed his hand and jogged across the yard, swinging his hand like they used to do on the way to the park. His laugh made this whole nightmare worthwhile.

"Do me a favor. Get on the bus and hang out the window. I want to take your picture." Christina waved her phone, and then pressed a kiss on Parker's forehead. "I'll catch you on the flip side."

Parker rolled his eyes as he did every time she said it, clambered up the steps, and then popped his head out the bus window. Riley was in the seat behind him, her eyes glued to whatever was on her phone.

Christina called, "Love you like pepper-oni pizza."

Parker answered, "Love you like choco-late ice cream." She snapped the picture in time to get his happy grin. Then the bus driver closed the doors and pulled away from the curb.

Before she could make herself crazy by weighing whether it was a good idea to humor Leanne or not, Christina quickly typed up a text.

Parker and Riley are headed home from school. Seem well.

She attached the photo and hit Send, then stood there staring at her phone, waiting for the answer, until the school yard was empty. When it was clear Leanne wasn't going to respond, Christina shoved her phone back in her pocket and headed for the bar where she'd worked until Leanne left town.

The money had been so much better there, but she'd never be able to make it into work from the cabin she'd "inherited" from her father. The Braswells had lived outside of Sweetwater ever since they'd made it over the mountains. The mule had probably broken down right there. Her mother had refused to stay there when he went to prison, and years of neglect had done nothing to improve the place. Over the years, the cabin had been updated here and there, but it was only a roof over her head. She'd had dreams of moving into town, getting one of the apartments springing up around the edges.

Now she'd have to buy a car.

As she walked into the Branch, she had her spiel all worked out. Instead of waiting for her to launch into it, the owner, a tough cookie named Sharon, snapped, "You'll work for tips." Late afternoon was a slow time for the large open building that served beer for the fishermen, white wine for their wives and a plain, tasty menu with reasonable prices. If the campground diner had plenty of charm, thanks to the natural beauty outside the large windows, the Branch had space. That was about it. Of course, after the sun went down, the crowd got rowdier and neon lit up the walls.

When she was young, Christina had loved it.

Now she was certain she didn't want to know why the floor was so sticky.

"I'll work for tips." Grateful, Christina caught the apron and said, "And a ride home at the end of the night."

Sharon narrowed her eyes. "Fine. I better stop drinking." She waved her usual mug of root beer and cackled like she'd made the most original joke in history.

Sharon never drank. But she owned a bar. Nothing Christina had ever done had convinced Sharon to tell her how that disconnect happened, not that it mattered. After a few dumb choices as a teenager, Christina was pretty firmly up on the no-alcohol bandwagon herself.

When she considered how nice it would be to have an escape at the moment, it was easier to understand Leanne's struggle.

"Better limber up your slappin' hand. The crowd seems restless lately, what with winter looming." Sharon handed her an order pad, a tray, and pointed her at a dark corner. "Haven't cleared the last table yet. While we're slow, see if you can make some progress. Any money you find is yours."

Since the bar wouldn't pick up for a couple of hours, there was no rush, but Christina was happier working than sitting around worrying about Leanne. After she finished clearing the table, which, judging by the leftovers and the generous tip, had come from tourists with a nice-sized bankroll, Christina caught the burger basket Sharon slid down the bar. "Better eat while you can. Keep up your strength."

Instead of arguing or offering her the tip money, which would have covered the most popular item on Sharon's menu, Christina took a bite of the greasy burger and sighed. Sometimes, life could get her down, but junk food renewed her spirits.

"Hear you're having a rough go." Sharon wiped the glasses at her elbow in assembly line fashion before stacking them. "You gonna pull out of it soon? I didn't hold your job, but I'll toss the new girl out if you're coming back full-time."

"Unless you're running a shuttle, I better stay out at the campground for now," Christina said slowly.

Sharon leaned against the counter. "Pretty girl like you, you could do better than either that place or this one. Find you a nice, decent man, settle down."

"I've seen how far that gets a pretty girl, Sharon. I'll keep working, thanks." Christina shoveled french fries in her mouth and tried not to think of her mother or Leanne, or even the dumb things she'd done to try to make some man love her enough.

Looks might catch a guy's interest, but she'd never succeeded in hooking the right kind of man.

"Beau was no loss, honey. You should have seen the fight he started in this place. Ugly temper." Sharon shook her head. "Older guy. One with some miles on him, but an appreciation for a pretty smile and some brains. That's what you need."

Beau had never been about forever. He'd been about distraction and wanting to pretend someone cared about what happened to her. He'd fixed that about three minutes after Leanne had shown up and told him she was ready to take him up on his offer.

If that was what happened. The timing could have been pure coincidence.

She needed to stop listening for the bits

of gossip she picked up during the morning rush.

More than that, once she got her car keys back, she needed to lock up the cabin and hit the road. There was nothing left for her here anymore. Leanne didn't care enough about her, either.

Parker's sweet face flashed through her mind. Whatever Leanne had screwed up in her life, her son was so kind and genuine that he was impossible not to love more than life itself. Saying goodbye to Sweetwater and the gossip and Leanne's mistakes would mean missing out on Parker's future.

But if Brett had his way, she'd miss most of it anyway. There had to be a path to pull the family back together. Maybe Brett was better off without Leanne. There was no maybe to it, especially if Leanne had slipped into her old ways.

Could Leanne ever be healthier or happier without Brett? Was running away her attempt at finding out?

But her kids... Didn't they need to know her?

Christina had spent most of her life with no father, but losing her mother... She gulped and tried not to choke on the last bite of hamburger. Grief still blindsided her sometimes. Both Riley and Parker needed a mother in their lives.

But what if she only brought them drama and disappointment? What then? Were Parker and Riley better off learning to live without Leanne?

Sharon snatched the burger basket off the bar and slid a root beer toward her. "Can't tell what you're thinking, but you're burning brain cells. Take a few hours away from the worry."

Sharon was right. Nothing she plotted could change Tuesday night at the Branch.

Part of the answer was easy enough. Brett was the key to everything. If she wanted to see Riley and Parker, or get Leanne some contact with her kids, which might help stabilize her, she had to work on Brett.

Apparently, he was traveling. That might give her some time for inspiration.

When the first group of tourists chattered over the threshold, fishermen fresh off a day on one of the local rivers or lakes by the looks of them, Christina tied a knot in her T-shirt to make sure her curves were easy to see, picked up her tray and put some swing in her step.

The rest of the night was a blur, and she was grateful Sharon kept her word about the ride home when Sharon's truck stopped in front of her cabin with a loud groan. "Twenty minutes out of my way," Sharon grumbled as Christina slowly got out of the truck.

"For nearly eight hours of free labor," Christina said as she stretched her legs and felt the solid weight of the cash in her pocket. "Can I do it again Friday?"

Sharon snorted. "Yeah. Still think you ought to find yourself a honey, get married and set up house somewhere."

Christina waved and unlocked the cabin door. One solid slam of her shoulder against the wood opened it with a loud squeak.

If she stayed in Sweetwater, she should think about fixing up the place.

With all her spare money lying around, taking up space, that is.

Once inside, Christina dropped down on the couch, toed off her shoes and draped one arm over her face. Getting to the campground on time would mean an early morning, but the extra cash she'd earned tonight was a nice start on the new car fund.

Before she could make herself brush her teeth or wash her face or peel off the gross clothes she'd been wearing through bacon grease and spilled beer, Christina was asleep. Only the alarm on her phone saved her from missing her shift at the restaurant completely. Running late, she hustled up the mountain.

When Woody rolled to a stop next to her, she nearly cried with relief. Every conversation starter Woody launched, Christina shot down, until she finally said, "Need my caffeine, Woody. I'll talk to you after the first cup."

He saluted with a happy grin and immediately began whistling a tune that was off-key enough that she couldn't figure out what it might be. If she'd had more energy, she would explain to him how early-morning whistling should be punishable by jail time, but because of him, she wasn't too late. Her admirer from Monday hadn't shown up and the view of the lake with the mountains behind, that drew all their visitors, was as beautiful as ever.

She refilled Woody's cup promptly and checked the time. They'd made it almost through her shift. It was clear he was hanging around with the hopes of being her chauffeur again. "Woody, you know I appreciated the ride you gave me yesterday. But I can't take advantage of you any longer." *You generous old coot.* "You saved me this morning. I can find my own way home. Walk will do me good." She stretched and realized she was telling the truth.

He studied her face for a minute before he slapped both hands on the spotless counter and said, "Guess I'll see if I can't get out on that lake and rustle the wife up some dinner, then."

Christina nodded. "That's the perfect thing. Every woman loves a man who provides." His shoulders straightened and he tugged his hat down, a man determined to prove his worth.

"You need a ride, you call *me*, Chrissy." He waited for her nod and she wondered how she'd gotten lucky enough to find her own knight in camo ball cap. Since he was the only man who'd offered her a hand without a long list of demands in return, Woody was quickly edging out the slim competition for the top spot on her list of favorite people. It would be easy to take advantage of his kindness, but she'd learned the hard way not to depend on others when she could take care of herself.

As soon as she'd rung Woody up and cleared the last of her tables, she stuck her head in the manager's office. "I'm out, Luisa, unless you need anything else."

"Nope, get going. Can't remember the last time you had three days off in a row," Luisa said as she brushed her dark braid back over her shoulder. "That's practically a vacation. Got any plans?"

"Not really." Christina wasn't sure she was all that happy about the time off, since money had become necessary as air, but given how she felt right now, she could sleep for days. "If something comes up, call me. I'll still pick up any shifts I can."

Otherwise, hitchhiking into town to beg for more work from Sharon would be her only option.

The thought of it made her tired.

By the time she walked back down to her

cabin, those days off might be completely necessary. Her blisters had blisters. She'd made a nice wad of cash, but the hustle was a killer. "See you, girl." Luisa handed her a check, and then turned to answer the ringing phone.

At some point, Christina need to fire up her laptop, do some hunting for a cheap car, but that would mean taking the long walk back up to the restaurant to use the Wi-Fi and she didn't want to contemplate that.

Walking down the two-lane road, she realized what a beautiful day it was. Large, old growth trees meant the road was shady, and there was little traffic. She was in no hurry. And she did some of her best thinking along this stretch. This was something she'd learned: walking soothed her. This area was perfectly calm. As she listened to the birds chirping, the anxiety quieted. She had cash in her pocket, a place to live and a solid job. Things had been worse.

Leanne needed her help, and Christina couldn't turn her back on those kids. With her free time, the solution of what to do about angry, self-righteous Brett Hendrix would appear. She hoped.

CHAPTER FOUR

THE FIRST PHONE CALL Wednesday morning was a surprise, but Brett had turned the ringer on his phone off while he listened to a lecture on the importance of diversity in hiring, so he didn't have a chance to answer it. There was no voice mail. He decided it wasn't an emergency and didn't duck out of the lecture.

The thing about both of the sessions he'd already sat through was that he understood the reasoning behind diversity and drug task force de-escalation training, but they were already pursuing both at the reserve. He was living it day to day. Were there any helpful hints or tried-and-true tactics proven to improve either? Not really.

He stifled a sigh as he studied the course outline for the next day of training.

The second time his phone vibrated with an incoming call, he turned it over to see the Sweetwater school district's number. He closed his eyes for a long moment. Parker's cough had turned into something more. Of course it had.

And the school was calling him instead of his mother. That was the course he and the principal had agreed on the last time this happened, but it was going to mean an inconvenient string of phone calls. He'd taken an inconspicuous spot in the back row out of fear that this might happen, so he quietly stepped outside.

He hit Redial and paced back and forth in front of the line of tiny windows looking out over the packed parking lot. Praying that his mother would be able to handle whatever the emergency was didn't help much, but it was all he had.

"Sweetwater Schools," Janet Abernathy chirped in her perky phone voice. "How may I direct your call?"

"Janet, it's Brett Hendrix. I assume Parker's developed a fever and needs to go home?" He crossed his arms over his chest and tried not to imagine how much stress this situation was going to cause.

"Oh yes, he's a sick little boy. Nurse says

he should go to the doctor." Janet sighed. "Honey, I tried calling your mama, too, but I didn't get an answer. That's why you got the double ring."

The thing about living in a small town like Sweetwater was that everybody was in everyone's business. Most of the time, that irritated him to no end. Sometimes it could be a help, though.

"I'm in Nashville for training." Brett pressed his fingers over his dry eyes and tried not to wish for a wife who would help out with things like this. That was wasting brainpower. "I'll get her on the phone and send her over."

"Okay, then," Janet said. "Right now, he's stretched out on the bed in the nurse's office, cold compress on his forehead, but I can tell he feels awful. He didn't even say thank you when I gave him his grape juice and that is not Parker." Her concern was sweet and easy to hear. If he could pick a grandmother out of a catalog for his kids, she would sound like Janet Abernathy in that moment: caring, steady, ready to jump in with both feet. "Should I call Riley out of class?"

That would be a big help if his daughter could be forced to care about anything other than her own aches. Five years ago, Riley had babied her brother like her favorite toy. Now Brett had a hard time imagining Riley would do anything other than make things worse. Besides that, she was a kid. It wasn't fair to expect her to take his place. "Not right now. Let me get my mother on the phone. If it will be any longer than fifteen minutes before she's there, I'll be in touch."

As he ended the call, Brett checked the time. Almost noon. Surely his mother was out of bed for the second time by now. She got up to get the kids out the door, and then went back to bed until a "reasonable" hour.

"This better be reasonable," Brett muttered as he punched his mother's number. The contrast between Janet Abernathy's sweet concern and what he expected from his mother was amazing in an awful way. Brett tried to clear his mind. When she didn't answer the first call, his annoyance ticked up a notch. His job was important, and this was a requirement for the promotion he'd lucked into.

On the third try, his jaw was locked so tightly with tension that it was almost impossible to speak when she answered by saying, "What is it? What is so important?" It didn't take two seconds to understand why she hadn't answered immediately.

"Are you at the casino, Diane?" Brett asked. Not that he needed to. Someone close by hit a jackpot, and he could hear the victory music and tinny sounds of fake coins hitting metal.

"I am, but I'll be home in time to meet the bus." Her quick answer was evidence that she'd spent some time considering what to say if he called.

The slur on the last word immediately sent Brett's anxiety into overdrive. "Have you been drinking?"

"Yes, but I'm done now. I'll be sober in time to meet the kids by three." His mother spoke carefully. She didn't want a lecture. He had no time to give one.

"Parker needs to be picked up now. Not at three. He's sick." Brett pressed his hand against his forehead as he immediately searched for another option. Leanne was gone. He was hours away. His mother would have time to sober up and collect the kids before he could make it back to Sweetwater, and that was if he drove the whole distance with sirens blazing.

If he did that, he might as well turn in his badge and gun because no law enforcement agency in the country would overlook an abuse like that.

Maybe Ash? If he called his boss, Ash would step up. That was the kind of guy he was.

"Listen, just…" Brett didn't even know what to say anymore. He hung up the phone with a click, sick with panic and the realization that whatever he did would mean he'd be facing the loss of his job.

Needing his boss to step up for babysitting duty would leave a permanent mark on his record, even if the guy was good through and through.

Brett paced closer to the door, one hand squeezing his nape. He scrolled through his phone, desperate for another solution. Janet Abernathy was so kind she'd step in to help, but could he ask an acquaintance to get his son to the doctor? Besides, she was at work with an important job to do.

When he scrolled back up and passed Christina's name, Brett cursed under his breath.

Parker loved Christina. Out of all the choices he had, his son would choose her, even above his grandmother. Christina had her issues, mainly a bad reputation she'd earned early and a worse attitude, but she'd always been magic with his kids.

He gulped hard as he hit her number. What would it hurt to ask? He'd owe her a favor. That was easy enough.

"Hello?" Christina said, suspicion clear in her voice. "It says Brett Hendrix, but the Brett I know wouldn't call me if he was on fire and I had the only bucket of water in town."

There it was, the reaction he'd expected. Reaching out to her was a mistake. Brett squeezed the phone hard and battled the urge to end the call with a quick jab of his finger.

"I need your help." His voice was gravelly, like the words were forced out around the brick wall he'd put up between the two of them. With this one call, he was weakening the protection he'd built for Parker and Riley. He hoped he wouldn't regret it. "Parker needs you."

"What's going on?" she said immediately. Every bit of sarcasm was gone. All Brett heard was alert concern. That was the kind of reaction he wanted from his mother. "What does he need?"

Christina would help. Somewhere deep inside, he'd known she would. Some tiny bit of relief trickled into his brain and it was easier to think.

"Parker is sick at school. I'm in Nashville and my mother's in Cherokee at the casino. The nurse thinks he needs to go to a doctor, but you could take a look at him when you get there and..." Brett cleared his throat. "Nope, I need you to pick him up and take him to the doctor." She didn't have kids. What did she know about fevers and making the decision to get professional help? It was better to get a trained person's opinion. He wouldn't trust Parker with anything less.

"Can you do that?" Brett heard the order lacing his tone. Putting a question mark on the end didn't change much, but it would prevent her from hanging up.

"Yes," Christina snapped. "Officer, I am on the job." Then she cursed. "But I don't have a car." He could hear the panic edging into her voice. "I'll call Woody. If he's not out on the lake, he's in town. It won't take long."

From the tension in her voice, he could tell she was doing the mental spinning he'd been doing before he'd contacted her. Between the two of them, they could come up with a solution. This was what he did, levelheaded planning. Why was it easier to do that with her than on his own? "What about my old truck? Can you walk over to the station and get it? How long would that take?"

He drove the reserve's SUV most places, but the beat-up truck he kept on hand was nice for heading deep into the woods. No scratches mattered, and he could get away. Keeping it felt too sentimental most days, but it might save the day today. "Keys are in the glove compartment."

"Okay, ten minutes up, and then I'm headed into town." Christina's voice was breathy as if she was already on the move. He appreciated the immediate response.

How nice would it be to have someone like that around all the time? Christina didn't complain or question; she moved. That was enough to ease some of his worry in that moment. If he had someone else like her in his life, he wouldn't be the only one shouldering every problem alone.

Then he realized that it was still Christina on the other end of the call. There were about six different ways she could mess this up. "Call me when you get to the school, please. I'll let them know you're coming. You aren't on the list, so it might take some talking on your part, but if—"

"Can't talk, Brett, I'm running up a mountain," Christina said before she ended the call. The return of her normal sassy tone was reassuring. He didn't have anything solved yet, but things were not so out of control as before. As he imagined her racing up the road to the station, he wondered what sort of reports the rangers might get about a crazy jogger and smiled.

Christina had never worried overmuch about what people said about her. That was a quality he should try to grow himself.

While he waited, Brett called the school.

Janet didn't sound any surer of his final solution than he'd felt staring down his only option, but she agreed to let Parker go with Christina. Then he peeked back inside the classroom.

He should gather up his stuff and hit the road.

There was no way he'd be getting what he needed or even what he could manage to sift through and find from these classes. Not now. He'd be worried about his son and his mother and the last-chance solution he'd dragged back into the mix.

Remembering Ash's serious face when he'd said it was time to finish the training or else made Brett pause with his hand on the door. Parker needed a doctor and a prescription. Christina could manage that. His mother would be home eventually. She loved her grandkids in her own way. He had a plan that could work.

But Christina was still in contact with Leanne. She'd mentioned a phone call the last time he ran into her. What if Christina seized this chance to do something crazy, like take Parker to Leanne, wherever she was now? When his wife had first run off, he'd refused to investigate. She'd always been wild. And she would do like she'd always done, turn back up when everyone least expected it, knocked down and desperate for help.

Leanne would always upset whatever normal life he managed to carve out.

Quitting the management class would be easy. He'd already postponed it twice because of upheaval at home. It would also derail his career. Ash had made it simple. He could fish or cut bait.

Half a second from throwing in the towel and forcing himself to come up with some other career choice on the long drive home, Brett stopped when his phone rang.

"I'm at the school. Parker's with me." Christina's voice was tight with anger. "He should never have been sent to school today."

"I figured." He closed his eyes and pressed his forehead against the cool metal of the door frame. "I'll head back as soon as I can. Can you stay with him until I get there?"

"We're headed into Gatlinburg right now." Christina cursed as the truck slipped its gears with a loud groan. "If this rust bucket makes it that far. I can't believe the situations I get myself in."

Brett understood her completely.

He'd never imagined he'd be a single dad, either.

"Yeah, I get that. Please, take him to the doctor, and then straight back home. If I hear that Leanne gets a visit or finds her way back into my house because of this, I will—"

"I don't know where she is, Brett. Save your breath and your threats for some other woman who isn't doing her best to get a sick boy some medication all the while driving a truck that should have been turned into scrap metal ten years ago." Christina cursed under her breath as the truck groaned again. "Sorry, Parks. I shouldn't have said that."

Since the truck provoked the same reaction from him until he worked the kinks out, it was impossible to be mad about her language. The fact that she felt it necessary to apologize to his son and explain why convinced Brett she had enough love for the kid to pull it off.

"Can you stay with him?" Brett repeated as he tried to calculate how long he'd be. "I'll be home by ten." He thought he could do that without breaking the law too much.

"Listen," Christina said before she paused, "don't do anything crazy. I hear your panic. Until I picked him up, I shared it. He's okay. I solemnly vow to do nothing other than what you've asked me to do. Do the right thing for you, Brett. I can handle this. Here, talk to Parker while I make this right turn."

Brett could see the crowded intersection in his mind. In that truck, she'd have to concentrate.

"Hi, Dad, sorry I'm sick." Parker's voice was husky, as if a cough or congestion had roughened it, but otherwise he sounded fine. "Diane thought it was allergies."

Yeah, she'd thought the same thing every time he'd had a cold himself. "No problem, bud. Aunt Chris is going to get you some cough medicine, some other stuff to help if you have an infection."

"I should be all better by the time you get home and we can go fishing." Parker's voice perked up, and Brett relaxed. His son wasn't dealing with the end of his career or the panic over finding reliable help or even the anger of his mother walking out. He was focused on one of his favorite things: fishing at Otter Lake with Brett. No matter what else happened in this world, his son was okay. He wasn't broken by being left in a school office all alone. He was okay.

"We'll see. Let me talk to Aunt Chris again. I love you, Parker." Brett dodged the crowd that poured out the doors of the classroom and eased back in to pick up his stuff. By the time their break was over, he could be on the road to Sweetwater.

"Everything is under control, Officer. I'll hang with Parker and Riley when the bus comes until your mother makes it home. There's no need to drop everything." Christina sighed. "That's what you're planning, right? To come back now because nothing and no one will be okay until you're back in control?"

The sting of her words might have hurt, but it was impossible to argue with them.

"If he was your son, you'd do the same thing." Brett wasn't sure he'd ever considered the question about what kind of mother Christina would be, but at this point, it was front and center. He'd watched her with Parker and Riley ever since they were born. She'd always been as fiercely proud of the kids and protective against any slights as Leanne had, but she'd never once walked away from them. She was saving him, even though he'd made it clear he wanted nothing to do with her.

Christina's loyalty to his kids was beyond reproach.

"I'll lose my job if I bail on this training session." As soon as the admission slipped out of his mouth, he regretted it. Giving her any sense of his weakness meant she'd have an opportunity to exploit it.

The silence on the other end of the call almost had him convinced it had dropped as she'd moved through the hills of East Tennessee.

He was prepared to end the call when she said, "Stay, Brett. Your mother and I have this handled."

He wanted to argue.

Nothing he could come up with would have sounded sincere.

"I'll pay you for babysitting them, Christina." Twice what she deserved, obviously. "You can name your price."

Her disgusted huff of breath prepared him. "I'm not going to charge you for getting to spend time with my niece and nephew, you stiff-necked, pompous..." Whatever she saw, hopefully his son's inquisitive face, stopped Christina in her tracks. "But I'm keeping the truck and the keys for...a week. It's the least you can do."

Brett blinked slowly. She was right. It was the least he could do. In fact, if he'd been a more generous person, he'd have already offered her that when he heard about Leanne taking her car.

She could have asked for the world in return for her help. At the very least, she could have bargained hard for Leanne. Instead, she was only asking for the one thing a good neighbor would easily loan to another.

What was wrong with him? When had he become so hard?

"Definitely. You drive the truck as long as you need it, but I'm going to help you with...something." He wasn't sure what she needed most, a car or money, and he didn't have much extra lying around the house, but he wanted her to understand how much he appreciated her stepping up.

"Can't stand owing me a favor, can you?"

Brett hoped Parker didn't hear the bitter tone of her laugh. They had so much history, all of it tangled and angry at this point. But she'd still come through when he needed her. How long would it take for the bad taste in his mouth over his complete lack of choices and the slight pinch of shame over how he'd cut her from his life in a self-righteous act labeled "protecting his children" to disappear?"

"You know me pretty well." Of course she did. They'd grown up together. She could exploit so many of his weaknesses if she wanted, anytime, but she'd had that power all along and never used it. "Guess that's something we have in common, the stubborn refusal to accept help."

It wasn't much in the way of a return volley, but he could live with it.

"Be prepared for payback. It won't mean writing a check, either. I don't want to sneak around to check up on Parker and Riley, not anymore." Christina ended the call before he could say anything else or give her orders on what to do at the doctor's office or when to call him. The rest of the class filed back into the room before he could hit the return button.

Then he realized what she'd said. She'd been sneaking around, visiting his kids behind his back? He would have sworn he knew everything happening with Parker and Riley.

He couldn't investigate that now. Brett had a choice. Either he could gamble his career and race back to Sweetwater to take care of the most important thing in his life, his family.

Or...

He could trust the woman he'd been treating as completely untrustworthy for years to take care of Parker. That would mean admitting to and dealing with his own mistakes.

As the instructor stepped back up to the whiteboard, Brett decided to live with the anxiety and the worry and settled into his seat.

Never once in the time he'd known Christina and Leanne had Christina gotten herself in the type of trouble she couldn't get out of. She would protect Parker with every hard lesson and clever trick she'd learned.

Living with the decision to keep his job instead of racing home to Parker would take some doing.

CHAPTER FIVE

"YOU STILL WITH ME, PARKS?" Christina said as she jerked to a stop in the parking lot of the closest urgent care place she could think of on the road down to Gatlinburg. Parker only knew that his doctor was in the city, but he couldn't remember his name or his office.

Riley hadn't answered her phone when Christina had tried sending up an SOS. Christina absolutely refused to consider calling Brett. He didn't think she could do this, and his comment about not turning this into an opportunity to let Leanne in had made her angry enough to spit. The thought hadn't occurred to her until he'd planted the seed.

If Leanne found out about this afternoon and that Christina hadn't called her or more, she would be angry. Christina tightened her hands on the steering wheel. She'd have to worry about that later.

"Yeah, I texted Riley that you picked me up and were taking me to the doctor." He paused and blinked before sneezing all over the passenger-side window. "Sorry." He raised his arm to wipe off the window, leaving behind a murky smudge that she had zero intention of cleaning herself. Brett's kids, Brett's truck, Brett's window. He could de-smudge it himself whenever she gave him the keys back.

"No problem. Let's get you inside." Christina would have staked what was left of her reputation on a diagnosis of the common cold, but she could imagine Brett's angry, disapproving frown if she went with her own powers of observation.

Parker climbed down out of the truck and walked inside, his shoulders drooping in an un-Parker-like way.

"Go sit down." Christina pointed him toward a seat in front of the television and smiled as he flopped dramatically down to loll in the chair. Both of the Hendrix kids were little miniature versions of their father, so it was nice to see the occasional proof that Leanne was their mother. That drama? So Leanne. It must drive Brett nuts.

"Go ahead and sign in. Here's the paperwork we'll need. I'll make a copy of your insurance card." The woman caged in the office behind the tiny window didn't even look up. She made pinching motions with her fingers as she stared at her computer screen.

"I, uh…don't have insurance." At least, she had no proof that Parker had insurance. Christina checked over her shoulder. She should have ignored her pride and called Brett for the pediatrician's address, but Parker was lightly snoring, pink dots of color filling his cheeks. "But I'll pay for the office visit."

If she could. The wad of cash she'd picked up at the Branch would have to stretch pretty far to cover it. Instead of arguing with her or offering her a solution, the woman slipped another form across the desk that clearly outlined the costs of the visit, and then raised both eyebrows. She was pretty sure Christina would bail, but she had enough money to cover it, so she passed the bills across the desk, ignoring the hard knot in her stomach at watching it all disappear. "After you fill out the forms, bring them back. We aren't too busy today, maybe ten minutes." Her phone rang and she turned away, satisfied that she'd done her job.

Christina walked slowly around the room as she filled out the paperwork, a combination of pacing and thinking and remembering things like Parker's allergies and his birthday and the only broken bone he'd ever had, the result of an overly ambitious tricycle jump. When he didn't stir until the nurse called his name, Christina was relieved she'd brought him in.

Parker only did running and jumping and full-tilt assault on polite noise levels under normal circumstances. He must be feeling rotten.

The doctor asked three questions total, prescribed over-the-counter antihistamines, decongestants, lots of liquids and as much sleep as it took to recover from the common cold.

Just as she'd suspected.

Being right was nice, but Christina had a feeling that when it came to caring for

Parker and Riley, she would always err on the side of caution. Most parents would, wouldn't they? It was one thing to suffer through a cold when she diagnosed herself. Watching the little tornado she knew and loved curl into the seat when they got back in the truck would have made her too anxious to last through the night.

"Parks, I'm going to stop at the pharmacy. Can you come in with me?" Christina asked as she rolled through Sweetwater. If she had more friends in this town, she would call for support. Brett's mother might be home, so she could take Parker there first, and then come back to town for medicine.

He slowly blinked his eyes open. "Do I have to?" Parker didn't whine, but there was a thin edge of it coming through his voice.

Christina didn't blame him, either. She could sympathize with the need to sleep and irritation at the people who insisted you wake up.

Riley would be getting out of school soon. Was she old enough to be responsible for them both while Christina went inside? At her age, Christina had spent every single day of summer alone while her mother worked.

But that hadn't been a good plan. That had been about necessity.

Christina checked the time again and decided to drive by the school. She'd ask Riley herself and make the best decision she could, based on the girl's answer. The truck sputtered as she eased over to the curb behind the short line of school buses. When Riley glanced in her direction, Christina waved wildly at her, desperate to get her attention. Since she'd once been a teenage girl, Christina was already wise to the "pretending not to see you" expression, so she laid on the horn until Riley headed toward her.

"I see you've added grand theft auto to your list of skills," the girl drawled as she crossed her arms over her chest. "What happened to the window? Gross. I'm riding the bus home." The determined jut of her jaw reminded Christina so much of Leanne that it was easy enough to make a decision.

"Nope, get in. I need your help." Ignoring her comment on the state of the truck's smudged window, Christina put the truck in Drive and made the "hurry up" hand motion.

"With a sicko and a criminal? No, thanks. When the cops catch you in this stolen vehicle, I don't want to be anywhere around." Riley bent her head in to stare down at Parker. "He looks...fine." The slight wrinkle on her forehead made Christina wonder if she was trying to convince herself.

"He's sick. He needs to be in bed. I have to stop and get him some medicine, and I don't want to leave him alone. So get in." Christina waved at the angry honk behind her. Another parent was ready to take her spot in the line.

Riley studied the bus before rolling her eyes. "Fine." She grumbled as she yanked open the door. Parker scooted over to rest his head on Christina's arm.

"Can we stop and get some french fries?" he asked, sounding like his old self.

"Chicken noodle soup. That's what you need," Riley said with a quick glance at Christina. "Mom would make you eat soup." She crossed her arms over her chest. "If she were here, but she is not. Thank you so much, Christina."

"It's Aunt Chris, Riley. Don't confuse me with Diane. And I promise you, your mother will be worried when she hears Parker was sick."

"Who's going to tell her? You?" Riley drawled. "Because Parker and I, we can't talk to her."

"That's not my fault, but…" She glanced down at Parker and the worried frown on his sweaty forehead. "We'll follow her advice anyway." As she eased out of the line, Christina could remember half a dozen times Leanne had nursed her through a cold with soup from a can. Riley was right. "We'll all have some soup."

Riley didn't argue, and Christina had to pretend not to notice when she reached over to take her brother's hand. When they were much younger, Riley had been determined to be Parker's guardian. She'd been bossy enough with Parker that Leanne had been able to step back and watch with amusement as Riley kept him out of trouble.

How nice it would be to have someone looking out for her. Leanne had been that person for Christina off and on for years. Brett had wanted to be the big brother she never had, but his concern had been so wrong. Too weird. She would never see him as a brother.

No brothers or sisters, her parents were gone, and her best friend had deserted her while possibly going off the deep end.

Christina would have time to feel sorry for herself later. She could cry over the loneliness and hurt and worry then.

Right now, she had two kids to get home and feed and nurse back to health.

Riley wasn't sick, but there was something going on, and if it wasn't fixed soon, she might do something to harm her relationship with her father and brother.

Something she might not ever recover from.

"All right, Riley. Do you want to shop or watch over Parks?" Christina asked as she dug the few remaining bills out of her pocket.

"You go. I'll stay." Riley tilted her chin up. "Make sure you get the right soup. And crackers. He likes crackers."

Christina studied her face. "Anything you want while I'm in there?" It was the perfect opening for the girl to unbend, and whatever it took, Christina would make it happen.

"They don't carry alcohol. Cigarettes? I'll smoke anything." Riley's mouth curled. She was ready for the outrage and had already learned the teenage ability to provoke for the fun of it.

"Got it." Christina raised her hand as she slid out of the truck. She was halfway around the truck when she realized a danger and trotted back to yank the keys out of the ignition. "Wouldn't want to have to walk home from here."

Riley's lips were twitching as she slumped back against the seat.

Would the girl steal the truck from the grocery store parking lot? Christina hoped not. She wasn't old enough for driving lessons, much less hitting the road.

But she was her mother's daughter and Christina was already one car short because she'd trusted the wrong person.

The store was packed, but she sliced through the crowded aisles as she grabbed things for Parker—soup, crackers and a few treats for them all. Math had never been her strongest subject, but she was aware that she was cutting her cash supply very, very close.

Crossing her fingers as she stood in line that she'd make it through without the embarrassment of having to ask the checker to take things off the total, Christina stared hard at the speckled linoleum.

"How is my friend Parker doing?" Janet Abernathy asked as she wheeled up a grocery cart. "He was not himself today. Get him to a doctor?"

Since few people sought her out, the conversation caught Christina off guard, but Janet's concern was easy to see. "I did. I'm grabbing a few things, and then I'll take him home and make sure he gets some rest." In a rush, Christina added, "Riley's out in the car with him. I wouldn't leave him alone." Why was she defensive? Nothing she did would change anyone's mind, not now.

Janet reached over to pat her arm. "Good thinking. I'm not sure what I would have done in the same spot. I was purely concerned when Brett told me he was all the way over in Nashville and that his mama…" She stopped and tried a pleasant smile. "Well, you know. That man, he needs some help. His mama said he was courting someone, couldn't tell me her name or much about her, but she was relieved he was ready to get hitched again. Somebody special to make the load easier, that's what we all need." She sighed as if she could picture someone who was making her own troubles lighter.

"Well, that's me. Here I am." Christina held out both arms so that there was no way to miss her. Janet's eyebrows rose. Christina decided her tone might have been too aggressive, so she softened it. "Making Brett's life easier, and boy, do I feel special." The person in front of her left, so she plopped down her items and watched the total anxiously as the numbers climbed. As soon as she went over limit, she studied the three bags of candy she'd added in a fit of charity and a wild attempt to buy Riley's love through appealing to her sweet tooth. Some other time.

This was a familiar spot and Christina hated it.

"You'll have to leave those off and…" Christina studied the bags at the end of the cash register. It was going to have to be the crackers. That was the only choice.

"Honey, don't you even worry about this." Janet waved a hand. "I'll pick up the extra. That Brett, I know he'd do the same for anyone in the same boat and I'm happy to do so. You go get his kids taken care of, you hear? And you tell Brett how happy I am for him, all right?"

Christina wanted to argue, but the checker put the last bags of candy in with the necessities, and then handed everything to her. She took the money Janet offered and was ripping off the receipt when Christina turned and held out all the cash she had.

"I wish I could argue against you paying for what I can't cover," Christina said after she'd gulped down her pride, "but I want all that for Parker and Riley. Take this and I'll bring the rest by the school when I have it."

Christina wasn't going to run any debts to anyone in this town. Folks hadn't helped when she needed it. She didn't trust any of them to hold one of her IOUs.

"Can't you consider it a gift? If not to you, then to my friend Parker?" Janet wrinkled her nose in a truly adorable way. "I mean it. Don't worry about a couple of dollars. Help someone else out when you get the chance and we'll call it even."

A couple of dollars. How many times in her life had a couple of dollars kept her awake at night? Too many times. She didn't need the charity.

"I'll bring it by the school." Christina turned to go and realized that even if she hated the gift, she could still appreciate it. "But thank you."

Janet nodded. "Sure thing, hon. You go take care of that family. All three of them are pretty special. Hope we'll be hearing wedding bells soon enough."

Uncertain what to say to being lumped in with the difficulties at Brett's house and truly shocked by the idea that there might be another woman in Parker's and Riley's lives soon or even someday in the future, Christina waved, picked up her bags and hit the automatic doors at a trot.

The truck was there. Riley and Parker were talking about something, their laughs drifting out of the truck as she opened the door, and some of the anxiety that had made it hard to breathe ever since she'd answered Brett's call eased.

"Good. You aren't out joyriding through Sweetwater," Christina said as she started the truck. "Here's the ciggies you requested." She pulled out the box of candy cigarettes that had prompted a short victory dance in the candy aisle.

Smart-aleck teens: 0. Lucky olds: 1.

She tossed them at Riley, whose lips twisted into a reluctant grin. "Okay. You got me."

The immense pleasure that came from winning against an unbeatable opponent and how Riley smiled, even if she didn't want to, was turning the day into a win. Begrudging respect was still respect, especially when a teenager was involved.

"Oh, I want one!" Parker tried to grab the box from Riley, but she held it over his head. "You're supposed to share."

"I got you something, too, Parks." Christina pulled out a small bag of the sourest cherry candy that she'd ever put in her mouth.

"Those are Riley's favorite," Parker

moaned as if he couldn't handle the terrible turn his life had taken.

"I know, but she likes to share, isn't that right, Riley?" Christina waited for the realization to cross both their faces. "You're too young to smoke. Both of you. You can't start smoking until you're ninety years old." She wagged her finger. "And if you tell your father I bought you any form of cigarettes, candy or otherwise, he will murder me, and then I will come back from the dead, haunt you by following you to school and tripping you in the hallway, so be careful."

Parker studied her face closely as if he was trying to determine how serious she was, but Riley's lips twitched and she met Christina's stare as she nodded. "Fine. We'll share."

She pulled out the tiny stick of sugar painted on the end and offered it to Parker. "I'll give you this in exchange for that bag of cherry bombs."

Before Christina could argue about the unfair exchange, Parker was handing over his bag of candy in exchange for a single candy cigarette. The kid had no sense of self-preservation at all. He was all about genuine kindness.

Someone ought to teach him better.

Christina held out the last remaining bag of candy: watermelon candy. Parker's favorite. "I will trade you that single cigarette for this bag of candy." She held it out of reach of his grabby hands. "You have to promise me you won't trade for any more cigarettes." Not that it mattered. Riley would give them to the kid because she knew that Christina didn't want him to have them. But she'd be on the lookout.

"Fine. Here." Parker thrust the candy cigarette at her, and then opened the bag, unwrapped one candy, put it in his mouth and leaned back with a sigh. "Feels good on my throat, Aunt Chris. You're the best."

Christina thought about popping the cigarette in her mouth to celebrate her victory, realized the number of people who would report such a sighting to Brett and tossed it in the grocery bag. She'd hold the crackers hostage and get the rest of the box from Riley.

She was ready to back out of the parking spot when Riley shoved the box of cigarettes her way. "Take these. I wouldn't want you to get an ulcer." Her words were garbled because both cheeks were puffed with candy.

Relieved, Christina took the candy cigarettes as she wondered how much damage she'd done to the kids' teeth with the bribes that had seemed like heaven-sent inspiration inside the store.

Then she let that worry fly right out the open window.

She was the aunt, and that was in name only.

No one expected the aunt to be about nutrition and not ruining dinner. And there was no one in Sweetwater who'd be shocked that she hadn't thought the whole plan through.

"Let's get you home. You have homework." There. That sounded parental and concerned and all those responsible things she imagined rolled off Brett's tongue like small talk.

"It's early, Chris. We have time." Riley didn't glance her way as she fiddled with the radio, but the teenage disdain dripped from every word.

But since one of those words had been part of her actual name, Christina didn't take offense.

"Fine. Soup. We all need soup." Christina had settled into a comfortable silence with Parker and Riley on the way home, so it didn't even occur to her to worry about what would happen when she met Brett's mother there. They'd barely interacted in the years she'd clung to the periphery of the Hendrix family, but that meant this conversation would be awkward.

As soon as the truck stopped, Riley opened the door and jumped out. She fiddled with her backpack and pulled out a set of keys. When she noticed Christina hanging back, she motioned with her chin. "Soup. You're making it."

"If your grandmother is home, she might have something better." Wasn't that what normal grandmothers did? Cook delicious meals that made the house smell like baking bread and chocolate chip cookies all the while their frilly aprons remained pristine. Since she'd never had one of those "normal" grandmothers, Christina had spent a lot of time with television grandmothers in her head, embellishing them because how awesome would it be to have someone in your life that was a combination of a fairy godmother and a cookie baker?

Riley's snort made her opinion clear. "If she's back from the casino, and she isn't, she's on the computer playing in a poker tournament or planning her next cruise or..." Riley settled her backpack on one shoulder. "She isn't cooking soup or anything else. Diane has pizza delivery on speed dial."

Christina shifted the bag of medicine and soup cans from one hand to the other. Was she going to go in? Of course she was. These kids needed someone looking out for them until their father got home.

"I can heat up the soup," Riley muttered as she made "give me" motions with her hands. "You can get back to your exciting life. Parker will be fine." Her expression had changed as she watched Christina. She expected to be let down.

The spear of pain that hit in the center of her chest nearly shocked a gasp from Christina. She'd seen the same hard certainty in her own eyes more than once.

Riley was too young to know that.

Parker? He was collapsed against the wall as if the waiting was too much for him. He wanted his dinner and his bed. It hadn't occurred to him that the world would let him down. That was worth the price of getting over her nerves about meeting Diane Hendrix inside that house.

"No one can open cans and heat up what's inside like I can. It's an old family recipe," Christina said as she straightened her shoulders. "Time to eat."

Riley waited for an uncomfortable second before turning to unlock the door. "It's not a big deal. I watch out for both of us enough, Chris."

The second time her name made it into the conversation strengthened Christina. That was who she was, Aunt Chris, the one who'd been fun when they needed it. She could be strong when it mattered.

"But you shouldn't have to, Riley." When the girl whipped back around, an angry retort on her lips, Christina understood exactly where it was coming from.

"My dad is doing the best he can." Riley glanced over at Parker, who was frowning as he listened. She had more to say, but she settled on "We're fine."

"I agree. He is. This time, I can help and I'm happy to do it. That's all I'm saying." Riley didn't believe her, but Parker relaxed.

"Open the door," he whined. "I want to go inside."

"Oh, shut it, you little bug." Riley opened the door and marched inside. Christina followed slowly and relaxed as she watched big sister guide little brother into one of the seats at the kitchen table. They argued. They were brother and sister, but there was still some of the care Riley had naturally been born with inside.

"Point me to the can opener," Christina said as she followed them. She'd wished for a chance to spend time with Parker and Riley. This wasn't how she'd imagined that would happen, but she was going to do her best to make the most of every minute.

CHAPTER SIX

BY THE TIME his Thursday class was finally over, Brett was nearly certain he'd wasted a full day of his life. There was no hope that he'd recall anything the instructor had covered because he'd alternated between checking his phone to make sure he had no texts and wondering if he should call someone in Sweetwater to look in on his kids.

In this case, no news wasn't reassuring. Before the daylong class had started, he'd called Riley to make sure that the house was still standing and no one had been thrown in jail.

When his mother heard that Christina had saved the day, she'd texted him to tell him she was going to take the opportunity for a mini vacation. She'd be home on the weekend unless he needed her to go back sooner.

It was a good thing she hadn't answered

the first call. His anger would have set her phone on fire. Leaving a calm message had been next to impossible, but he'd managed it.

All he could imagine was every way Christina could destroy his life. Even if she didn't mean to, she could do so much damage.

He pulled his phone out and dialed her number. "Hello?" she answered breathlessly. There was the muted song of a commercial that played on a near-constant loop in the background. Either she was a fan of the annoying video clip show that ran on the kids' channel on Thursday nights, or she was still at his house. Parker never missed his chance to watch.

"You're still there. No sighting of my mother, then." He wasn't sure what he expected, but being let down like that was hard to handle. Doing it while he was separated from his kids by hours and miles was next to impossible. Brett leaned back on the motel bed and tried to figure out what he'd do about the rest of his life.

"Not yet, but everything is under control. Riley has disappeared to her room. I hear pop songs and occasional giggles, so I assume she's on the phone." The question in Christina's voice matched his feelings every time he paused outside his daughter's room and tried to imagine what sort of life she lived when she wasn't terrorizing the people related to her. It sounded like a lot of fun.

"Parker's cough has almost disappeared. He's stretched out on the couch with the remote in his hand, so I'm betting he's going to make a full recovery."

"Good." The smile he heard in her voice untwisted the worried knot in his chest. Then he realized the conversation was lagging. "I'm glad the patient's on the mend. And you? Are you okay? No cold?"

"Not yet. Thank you for asking." Then she snorted. "We aren't all that good at polite small talk."

She was right, but he hated it. "I know. I just…" What? What did he hope to accomplish? "I miss them. I guess I wanted to make this a longer call."

"By pretending concern for me," she drawled. "What a nice thing that is."

For some reason, her tone settled him,

returned him to firmer ground. "You don't handle actual concern well, as I remember." As always, the trickle of pleasure he'd enjoyed anytime he tangled with Christina hit and he paused to enjoy it. Their conversations had always been sparring, never the life-and-death matches he and Leanne entered. "Don't tell me you've changed."

Christina sniffed. "I've cooked dinner and done laundry and checked homework. I'm becoming domesticated after all. And you said it couldn't be done."

"Never said it." Brett kicked his shoes off, more relaxed than he had been in weeks.

"But you thought it. And that's okay. I never would have predicted how much I enjoy the Hendrix family routine, either." She lowered her voice to whisper, "Except for this annoying television show."

Brett closed his eyes and laughed. "Yeah. It's the worst. All reasonable adults agree."

"Glad I made the team this time," Christina said. He could hear the lightness in her voice and some fatigue. He knew that nighttime exhaustion that hit after a long day of parenting. He'd been building his endurance for years now. Christina had jumped into the deep end. He owed her.

"I'm really sorry. I wish I was closer, but I've got to finish this class. I've been putting it off for months. Ash basically gave me an ultimatum and I can't afford to lose this job. Strangely, I can't afford to keep it, either. And I'm not even getting that much out of it, except today we talked about new tech, so that was interesting, and I have some suggestions to make to the chief ranger when I get back. I'd be right to leave now. And my mother..." There were no words to explain how often she'd let him down. This was the worst so far. He would never be able to trust her again.

"That is a lot of words to chew on, Officer. Just wait a minute."

He listened as she said something to Parker that he couldn't quite make out. The sound of the television show grew faint, and then he thought he heard a door open and shut behind her.

Then the call of the tree frogs behind his house was all he could hear until the quiet squeak of the chains on the old porch swing on his deck kicked in. Homesickness washed over him. He'd rocked on that swing so many nights, just him and Riley as they stared up at the starry sky. Parker could never be still long enough to enjoy the night, but he and Riley could sit there together and just be.

Or they had been able to until the family had imploded, divorce had made him short-tempered and Riley so, so angry.

"You need to calm down, Brett. Everything is fine here. I promise. I can stay until Diane gets here." Christina was quiet for a minute, but the squeak of the old swing made it easy to wait for whatever she had to say next. If he couldn't be there, the sound of home made everything better. "If you want me to stay after she gets home, I'll do that, too." But she didn't want to. Her grim tone was proof of that, but he didn't blame her. It was no fun to share a house with someone who didn't want to be there.

He'd been doing that for a long time, first with Leanne, and then with his mother.

"I appreciate that, Christina." Brett got up to look out the window. Here the stars were impossible to see. Light pollution turned the night sky into a dull, yellowish blanket with only tiny pinpoints of light coming through.

"Really, there's nothing to be worried about. Finish your class. Parker and I were lazy bums today while Riley was at school. I have tomorrow off, too, so if he needs to stay home from school, we're covered." Christina cleared her throat. "I'm enjoying spending time with Parker."

"But not Riley. I get that." Brett ran his hand over his forehead. "I don't know what to do about it."

"We made some progress on the first day, but things have returned to a standoff. Except for dinner. She does not turn down food." Christina laughed. "A girl after my own heart."

He leaned a shoulder against the window. "I'm scared for her. For them both. I should quit my job." Why was he telling her this? He had no idea. Being away from home and worried sick over his kids had softened his brain.

"I had her for half a second in the car ride home. All it took was a sick Parker, a reminder that she used to care for him like a baby and some candy cigarettes. She smiled at me." Christina cleared her throat. "My plan is to build on that."

"Candy cigarettes? Why would you think that was a good idea? Did anyone see her with them? Because how will they know they were candy? What will people think of my teenage daughter rolling through town with a cigarette dangling from her mouth?" As soon as the last words tumbled out, Brett could hear how loud he'd gotten. Worry and frustration and a million different fears were hard to control in this stupid motel room. Was his job worth losing his kids? Of course not. He turned to grab his suitcase. He'd pack and hit the road. Ash could give him a pass for partial credit or not, but he had to get home.

"Well, not to add to the shouting volume, but if I'm staying tonight, people are going to be scandalized that I'm in your house. I also spent every last dime I had on a doctor for your son, fed both of your kids and had a close encounter with a fine, upstanding Sweetwater citizen when I was buying said cigarettes. If you're worried about the opinions in this town, you've already got some extensive mopping up to do. Might as well keep your job, you pompous jerk."

Brett bit back the angry response that bubbled to his lips. All she was doing was helping him. Maybe his concerns were those of a parent and she had no reason to understand that. She was still doing him a favor that he'd have to repay.

"I'm sorry. Thank you for everything you did yesterday and today. My mother…" He wasn't even sure what to tell her. The fact that she wasn't answering his calls was a bad sign. "I don't know what to say."

"Are you worried about her?" Christina asked, her voice calmer. "Want me to call the police? I'd head over to the casino, but the kids…"

Brett closed his eyes. Even though they'd been half a second from yelling at each other seconds earlier, Christina would still help him if he could think of anything to do. That was one of the main differences between Leanne and her best friend. Christina had always been ready to fight, but her anger disappeared as suddenly as it boiled over. Leanne would nurse the anger until there was nothing but cold silence between them and it seemed impossible to get back to where they belonged.

"Brett, tell me what to do to help and I will." Christina also never took the easy way out. If Leanne wanted to get out of something, she'd change the subject. Christina faced everything head-on. "She's your mother. I know you're mad, but she is your mother."

She'd tried that same argument with him about Leanne. It was a strong argument.

"I'll call Ash, get him to call up a few friends in law enforcement. They can check the casino. I'm sure she's still there. Probably hit a winning streak or found some old friends or..."

The rattle of the door opening interrupted the string of excuses he was making and it was a relief.

"She just walked in. Your mom is here." Christina was as relieved as he was, but she didn't have the eruption of anger in her gut.

"I want to talk to her." Brett inhaled and exhaled slowly as he listened to the muffled conversation. He wasn't sure how Christina would react to his mother, but she was strong enough to stand up to questioning if she had to. Right now, he had to say what was burning inside.

"I know you're mad, but everything is fine," his mother said instead of a useless greeting that no one wanted to waste time with. "I'm not sure why you ever called her after all the trouble Leanne has put you through, but you did and it was nice to have a break. For now, I'm here and I'll stay until you get back."

What Leanne had put him through. Her way of summing up years of turmoil was short and to the point. The resentment that had been building ever since his mother had handed over her ultimatum moved up to a boil.

"You ought to know something about that turmoil, I guess," Brett snapped before he closed his eyes and tried counting to a million to calm himself. He didn't have much room to maneuver here. "I need to know I can count on you, and I don't."

The silence on the other end of the call made it easy to hear the frogs croaking away, the continuity and reliability of that noise tied closely to home. Why couldn't he have that same comfort when he heard his mother's voice?

"I put my life on hold to come back here to help you—"

"And I appreciate that, Diane." Brett ground his teeth together at the stupid concession. "I definitely need you, but if I can't depend on you all the time, I can't depend on you any of the time."

His mother huffed out a disgusted breath. "How long is this living arrangement going to last, Brett?"

He pressed a hand against his forehead. "They'll be my kids forever. What kind of question is that? You know how old Parker is. I'll need help for years."

She didn't answer, but they both knew how she felt about that. "It's time for a change, then."

Her quiet words were the hammer he'd been waiting to strike. She'd made it clear from the start that this solution was temporary. His time had run out.

"Let me get home from Nashville. I'll do...something next week. Can you wait for one more week?" Brett asked, even as he wondered what the point might be of continuing the classes at the law enforcement academy. There was no way being a cop, with the odd hours, would work if being a ranger for the reserve was impossible, but Ash might have a suggestion. Brett had to exhaust all of his options before he gave up the job he loved.

"Sure. One week. And I'll ask around town to see if anyone can recommend a nanny." His mother cleared her throat. "But a wife, a good, steady woman who dreams of having a family is what you need. That's the only thing that will make you happy."

As if she had any idea what might make him happy. Saying that would only fray their relationship further. "Let me talk to Christina."

He wasn't sure what the holdup was, but eventually Christina answered. "She's gone. You tell me what you need me to do and I'll do it. The nerve of that woman is… Well, I've never seen anything like it and I've seen some nerve. These kids need her and she decides she doesn't want to be here? I mean, really, who does that?"

He'd never expected to appreciate Christina as an ally, but in that moment, she was saying everything he desperately wanted to and it felt good to not be so alone in the world.

"We both know two women who have done exactly that," Brett said quietly, exhausted all over again at how decisions he'd made could go so wrong. Over and over, he faced the consequences of mistakes he'd made as a kid. He loved Riley and Parker both so much that he'd never regret getting tied up with Leanne, but if he could go back in time, he'd tell young Brett to run fast and far away from a girl who'd trump his mother for being selfish and undependable.

Christina sighed. "Yeah. We do." He heard the quiet squeak of the swing and could picture her sitting there on the shadowy deck in the spot he loved so much.

"I learned early to take care of myself. My kids will know they can rely on me. I'm coming home as fast as I can get there. I'll leave as soon as I pack. If you want to head home, take the truck and keep it for as long as you need it, Chris. I'm sorry I dragged you into this mess."

She cursed softly. "Seriously? You think

I'm going to leave after your only other choice for responsible adult has flaked on these kids already? Nope. I'll wait until you're here. I may have to sleep on this swing if she locks me out of the house out of concern for all your valuables, but that's okay. I've gotten used to sleeping where and when I can. And you're right. I'm driving that truck." She was silent, but he could almost hear the words rolling through her brain as she carefully weeded through them. "You know, Brett, I've got a lot of annoyance with you built up. Years of irritation, stacked up like firewood waiting for a match, but the fact that I've been shut out of this family until you need me?" She exhaled loudly. "Well, I get it. I get that. You're protecting your kids. Don't you ever apologize to me for asking me to help them, though. I love Riley and Parker. I always have, no matter how dumb you've been, and I always will, no matter the trouble Leanne causes. I love them. Don't apologize to me for giving me a chance to have what I want."

Brett eased down on the side of the bed, ashamed all over again at the way he'd treated Christina. He'd thought cutting her out of his kids' lives would keep them safe. What he'd done instead was cut one of the few strands of his own safety net.

"Fine. I'll apologize for acting like a jerk, then." He flopped back on the bed. If he survived this day without dying from a whiplash of roller-coaster emotions, it was going to be a miracle. "But don't expect me to be any good at it. I'll need practice."

"I'd ask you to repeat yourself, but until I see the words coming out of your mouth, I'm never going to believe that you haven't been replaced by aliens. Brett Hendrix doesn't apologize. I can find a whole list of people who will testify to that fact." Her voice had relaxed, some of the tight anger gone.

No matter how he tried to tell himself she was exactly like Leanne, Christina continued to prove him wrong. She was different, easier to talk to, and he needed that right now.

"All right. I'll owe you an apology when I get back. If you're sure you don't mind, please stay with my kids until I'm home. I don't know that I'll have any magical solution then, but I don't want to give up yet."

Christina laughed. "You know, most of the time, I'm pretty certain we're different species, but then you say things like that. You don't want to give up, not yet. So many times I've thought that to myself."

She'd had some pretty big battles to fight on her own. Of course she understood not going down without a fight.

"I don't know what your work schedule is for next week, but if you can help..."

Brett had no idea what to even ask for.

"I will help. The thing about people expecting the worst of you is that, if you're irresponsible, nobody's surprised." The tough edge was back. "Riley and Parker may be having breakfast out at the campground, but we'll make this work."

Brett did his best to relax his tight shoulders. He had about a million orders to give her to make sure his kids were fed right and did their homework and stayed away from the television shows they begged to watch but he refused, and then there was the whole dangerous issue of their mother, where she was and what she might want.

But he couldn't. The weight of the world was too much sometimes and he had to let go.

"Brett, you can trust me. I've got this. With Riley's help, the house will still be standing when you get back and both of your children will be fine."

"Promise me you won't bring Leanne in while I'm gone." Brett squeezed his eyes shut, afraid that this would be the second he lost everything.

Her long silence was the only answer until he heard her settle in the squeaky swing. "I don't know where she is or what she's doing. Because of that, I'm afraid to tell her anything about this."

He studied the shadows on the ceiling as he considered that. "You don't trust her?"

"With my life, yes," Christina responded immediately, "and if she were still here and I'd seen her yesterday and the day before, I'd know whether I trusted her with Parker and Riley, but she isn't, so I don't. Until she comes back home, you can relax about my motives here."

"No sneaking around?" Brett asked.

"I guess that'll be up to you. It always

has been, but I love them. She loves them. Only a fool would expect it to be easy to keep us away from them."

Brett realized he understood exactly what she meant. If he could put himself in her shoes, as an innocent man, he'd do whatever it took to see his kids. "Okay. We have an agreement. When I get home, we can discuss...everything else."

"You concentrate on becoming the best upstanding officer of the law you can be. Things will be under control in Sweetwater."

The dig at his job came as a surprise, but he'd used it often enough to excuse cutting her out of his family's life that he acknowledged he deserved it.

"Thank you, Christina." There was nothing left to say. He couldn't fix years of bad behavior while he was hours away and she'd fight him on it anyway.

"You're welcome. Do you want to talk to Riley or Parker?" she asked quietly.

He did. More than almost anything he wanted to talk to his daughter and son, but the homesickness might drag him under if he did. "No, I'll call in the morning. Everyone needs their rest tonight."

"I better get inside before your mother realizes she can lock me out," Christina said. He imagined a smile on her lips and hoped she was teasing him.

"Good night."

He said goodbye and released a long, pent-up breath. He had the time he needed to finish the class required to keep his job. That was one hurdle he could clear with Christina's aid. After some sleep, he could come up with solutions on how to keep jumping the next hurdles all alone.

CHAPTER SEVEN

THE THING ABOUT growing up the way she had was that Christina had no concept of how to deal with a family meltdown like the one Brett and his mother were currently experiencing. She hadn't had much family to worry about, and Leanne had never been stable enough to lean on for long.

Christina propped her feet up on the arm of the swing and considered her choices. The easiest thing to do would be to go home for the night, and then come back in the morning. If she could trust Riley to call if Diane left, she'd do that. Having her in the house would cause more friction. Riley would be forced to find something snarky to say every time they ran into each other in the kitchen. That would upset Parker. And Diane Hendrix would still be wearing the puckered lips that clearly demonstrated her distaste.

But there was no way she was leaving Parker alone. Not yet. And she'd insisted to Brett that she could do this. So she would.

As she swung her legs down to the weathered wood of the deck, Riley peeked out the door. "Is Diane out there?"

Christina shook her head. "She's inside somewhere."

Riley checked over her shoulder, and then stepped outside. "Was there an epic shouting match?"

"It wasn't pretty," Christina said, "but I only heard one side of it." And that had been enough. One thing that filled her with immediate rage was a mother who couldn't be bothered. Kids crying "MommomMom-momMom" in the grocery store while Mom chitchatted on her cell phone were nearly impossible to ignore. She'd learned early on that her own mother didn't appreciate that neediness, but she hated that other kids would have to learn it, too. If it came down to an epic battle between the uptight know-it-all who'd made her life difficult and the woman who'd made him the way he was, Christina would always come in on Brett's side. It was a blind spot, but she wasn't going to fight it.

"Yeah, usually there are few words, but all the oxygen is sucked right out of the room. At breakfast. Every day." Riley kicked the post holding the deck railing. "It's almost like Mom's back home." She didn't glance over her shoulder at Christina, but she seemed a weird combination of warrior with militant shoulders and a tiny girl who had no call being so tough. Riley was being broken by this divorce. Christina hated that, but how could she help?

"Guess I'll be camping out on the couch for a bit." She might as well make it clear that there was no room for argument. "Want to help me pick Parker up and put him to bed?" One of the sweetest memories she had of Parker and Riley was when he was still a toddler and Riley insisted on reading a book to him every night. The first time she'd seen the little girl squinting hard at the pages of a book and sounding out words while a little boy stared up at her, Christina's heart had shattered. That was what she'd always wanted, someone to look out for her and someone to worship. Parker could have that, but only if Riley had support.

"Kid's like a sack of potatoes. I'm not sure either one of us can lift him now." Riley kicked the post again. "You can go home. I'll be here." She wrapped her arms tightly over her chest. "We'll lock the doors. Diane won't leave until Dad gets back home, and even if she does, we have plenty of groceries."

The fact that she'd done so much planning on what she'd do if she were left in charge made Christina angry all over again. Just because she could take care of herself and her brother if she had to didn't mean that it was right that a young kid was worrying herself over such things.

"No way. Miss out on the cushy cable package and a full refrigerator?" Christina snorted. "It'll be like a vacation if I stay here, couch or not. My cabin has four walls and a door that locks, but no one would volunteer to stay there if they had a choice." It hurt to say that, but it wasn't far from the truth. Her inheritance was falling down around her ears, but it belonged to her.

"Suit yourself. Grown-ups always do." Riley turned to go inside and Christina could see her chance to change their relationship slipping away.

"Thank you for your help this week. I know you're mad at me, but I needed a hand." Christina tipped her chin up. "You didn't have to do that. I know you did it because you love Parker."

Riley pursed her lips. It was easy to see the warring urges of little girl and surly teenager on her face. "I do. But I didn't do much."

Their eyes met in the dark shadows of the deck. "I'm doing the best I can, Aunt Chris, but it isn't enough."

Tears surprised Christina, but only for a second. Then she was out of the swing and had her arms wrapped around Riley's stiff shoulders. "Honey, you're doing more than you should, and don't you ever think any different. You should be laughing with your friends and singing pop songs at the top of your lungs and worrying about who likes whom in the seventh grade." But how could she convince the girl that was the truth? With the way things were in the Hendrix house, Riley would always be called on to be more mature than she was. With her mother and Brett's family, Riley was facing a stacked deck. She'd have to grow up fast.

Christina knew what that was like. Once people expected her to make adult decisions, it was awfully hard to stop. When she was forced to take care of herself, adults lost the ability to force her to go to school or listen to all their rules.

When Christina should have been studying geometry and *Romeo and Juliet*, she'd been honing her shoplifting skills with grocery smuggling and ducking the police. She and Leanne had skipped so much school Christina's sophomore year, she'd been lucky to pass.

At too young of an age, Christina had come to understand that her mother couldn't stop her from drinking at the lake with her friends or riding shotgun in a car Leanne had borrowed for a day trip to the mall in Knoxville whenever they felt lucky and fearless enough to test mall security. The freedom had been overwhelming.

Brett's daughter was already carrying more responsibility than she should. When she realized that and started pushing hard against her boundaries, Riley would come to the same understanding, not as quickly as Christina and Leanne had, because Brett was there. But she was losing precious time to be a kid.

That was the danger that had to keep Brett awake at night.

"That's kid stuff. I don't have time for that," Riley muttered into her shoulder before she stepped back. "I've got to get my mother to come home and figure out how to make my father back into a human being, and then Parker…" She shook her head. "Doesn't matter. We don't need you, Aunt Chris. You can go home. I've got this."

She was back inside before Christina came up with any words. They weren't the right words, so it was easy enough to swallow them.

After one last glance at the clear night sky, Christina went indoors. Riley was bent over Parker, rousing him from sleep. Christina watched as Riley guided him down the hall to his bedroom. The quiet sound of two doors closing echoed in the living room and she missed the annoying kids' show that had been slowly driving her out of her head before Brett's phone call.

As she stretched out on the couch, Christina thought of all the things she had to figure out. She'd missed a prime opportunity to reseed her car fund by skipping the happy hour crowd at the Branch. Since she was back to zero now, that hurt.

But she was going to sleep on Brett's couch, and in the morning she'd face off against his mother and she'd let Leanne know about Parker's illness and his recovery.

Until she fell asleep, she'd consider ways to help Riley and Parker. There had to be something she could do to regain her spot on the fringes of the family. Brett was at his weakest point. She had to capitalize now if she had any hope of regaining any access for Leanne in the future.

That would take some time. When she found the answers, she'd know whether it was a good idea to bring Leanne back into the fold.

Thinking of Brett made it easy to picture him in a hotel room, staring up at the ceiling while he wrestled with the same problems.

And he'd been doing it for so long, all alone. On the outside, things had seemed so different, but Brett had been faced with the same problems she and Leanne had. They'd learned to look out for number one, while Brett was doing his best to save the world, one annoying order at a time.

Understanding his burden better made it impossible to hold on to all of her anger. When he got back, it was time to consider how they could work together. Christina curled comfortably into the cushy couch and tried not to fixate on how easy it would be to get used to the Hendrix home.

AFTER TOO MUCH time spent as a stranger in a small house packed with two kids and an angry retiree, Christina was glad to get back to work. Parker said he was ready for school. Luisa had a shift for her, and if she spent another day in the Hendrix house, puttering around and cleaning out shelves or the refrigerator to fill her time, she might never leave. It was nice to have a home.

If she could get Riley and Parker dressed and out the door on time, she'd lure them to the diner with promises of bacon. Then all

she had to do was convince Luisa that taking a twenty-minute break right in the middle of the breakfast rush was completely logical.

She'd done much more difficult things, but she wasn't entirely certain that she was ever going to get the kids moving.

"Come on, Parker, I can't be late and take you to school all on the same morning," Christina muttered as she thrust the missing tennis shoe at the little boy, who was brushing his teeth while he blinked sleepily.

"It's too early, Aunt Chris. I can't eat until I'm awake," he said before spitting into the sink.

"I know it's early. And when your dad is back, you won't have to come with me to the diner to open, but for now, try to concentrate on hot pancakes." She stuck her head out the door. "Riley, in the truck. Now!"

"I'm waiting on you." Riley was leaning against the front door. "It's not every day I get to leave the house two hours before I have to be at school. I wouldn't want to miss a thing. It's so exciting." Her dull tone

matched the expression on her face. She was dressed head to toe in drab green, almost as if she needed camouflage to make it through the day.

"Your dad—"

"Right. He'll be back tomorrow and we'll be on our normal schedule. You've said that. Over and over. Who are you trying to convince, us or yourself? Babysitting wearing you out?" Riley rolled her eyes. "I can get us on the bus on time. I do it every morning that Diane's here anyway."

"But you shouldn't have to." Christina could remember waking up alone and walking down to the bus stop by herself. Leanne had always been the type to chase down the bus as it was leaving. Waiting drove her crazy. Christina had been determined that no one would have to make a special effort for her. The town expected the worst, even when she was a kid. She'd give them no extra ammunition, then or now.

"Everyone, load up." Christina waved her arms in the air, urging both kids toward the door. "Diane is sleeping in. Do you want to tell her goodbye?" They'd

danced uncomfortably around each other long enough. Brett's mother hadn't wanted her in the house, but she wanted to be in Sweetwater even less, so she'd quietly disapproved. Since she could have locked the door and forced Christina to crawl in the window over the kitchen sink, Christina was happy enough at the hostile truce.

"She'll text us from the road. Diane's not big into mushy goodbyes." Riley yanked open the door and marched down the sidewalk. Parker dragged his feet, but he made it out into the predawn morning finally and Christina closed the door. She twisted the knob to make sure it was locked before realizing she'd have no means to get back in after her shift was over.

And that was fine. Sharon would let her hang out at the Branch and serve any of the late lunch crowd before she picked the kids up from school.

It was almost like she was a real mother.

Except she was dragging them out to a campground diner before the sun rose and contemplating killing time at a bar before she met them at the end of their day.

"Fine. I'm a mother with two jobs. Even

more impressive," Christina muttered as she started the truck.

Neither kid seemed interested in conversation and Christina was relieved to see that she was only five minutes late as she pulled into the parking lot. She urged them to hurry into the diner, and then pointed at two seats at the end of the counter. "Sit there. Breakfast is coming."

She scribbled two orders down and handed them through the window. "VIP order, Monroe."

The kid waved a spatula and turned away to get more bacon.

Woody waved his coffee cup. "Been waiting on my favorite waitress. Luisa took my order, but I knew you'd be here soon." He raised an eyebrow and motioned with his head toward Riley and Parker. "Got a couple hitchhikers this morning, I see."

Christina poured his coffee with one hand while she tied her apron with the other. "Yeah. Helping out while Brett's in Nashville for training."

Woody slurped his coffee while he studied Parker and Riley. Both were propped against the counter, chins on hands while they blinked sleepily. If she were a real mother, she'd be terrible at it. They were kids. They needed rest.

"That Leanne." Woody shook his head sorrowfully the same way she'd watched other good people from Sweetwater do over the years. "What is she doing to those kids?"

Riley immediately straightened and Christina knew the girl could hear every word Woody was saying.

The first time the owner of the convenience store next to the highway caught her pocketing beef jerky she'd planned to eat instead of the expensive cafeteria lunch she couldn't afford, two women had stopped him from calling the police. They'd blamed Christina's mother for her wildness.

"How can she know what's right? Her mama never brings her to church." Christina could still remember the syrupy tone and the burning anger that had kicked up in her gut. Her mother had worked whenever and wherever she could and still struggled. All alone.

Being poor was no crime, even if some

people wanted to treat it that way. Her mother had been the innocent one.

Christina remembered the burning embarrassment that inevitably came with the pity that people were happy to shower even when they never offered help, so she immediately got angry. "You know, Woody..." His shocked expression convinced her to pause. Anger wouldn't change anything. "It's easy to think you know what's going on, but most people are doing the best they can with what they have." Parker and Riley would have done better with an extra hour of sleep. Today, they'd trade that for a good breakfast and a view of the sunrise clearing the valley mist off Otter Lake.

Woody slurped thoughtfully. "How'd you make it into work, Chrissy?"

Riley wrinkled her nose at the nickname; Christina, grateful someone else heard it and agreed with her that an adult woman deserved better, blinked slowly. "I drove."

The girl's lips curled and she eased off the stool to take the plates Monroe slid in the window. "I've got these, Aunt Chris."

Both kids were silent as Christina fell into the diner's rhythm. She took orders and delivered them, rang up customers' bills at the cash register and pocketed tips, all the while she refilled drinks and did her best to smile happily. The fact that so many of the morning faces were locals bothered her. The way gossip traveled in this town, she might be facing a visit from the police for kidnapping Leanne's children.

The fact that Leanne would fully support that plan might explain some of the concern, as long as Christina was kidnapping in order to bring Parker and Riley to her, but it was more likely that years of always being caught in the crosshairs of the good people of Sweetwater had left her with a bit of a complex.

Mornings were usually busy. Everyone was easing into the day, not lurking in the hopes of seeing something exciting.

Why didn't that sound reasonable?

"Luisa, I'm going to run the kids in to school. I'll be back in fifteen." If she broke all the speed limits, she could do it, too. Riley had Parker nearly out the door by the time Luisa reluctantly nodded. "Tomorrow, Brett will be home and everything will be back to normal."

"So you'll be fifteen minutes late, but you'll stay for the whole breakfast rush," Luisa said. "It works. I've got this covered."

"Can you fill 'er up before you go?" Woody asked as he pushed his coffee cup forward.

"I've got it." Luisa waved the coffeepot and frowned at Woody. As the manager, Luisa stressed the importance of excellent customer service. It was nice to see her dealing with a difficult diner. "Go on now."

Christina had no time to express her irritation or gratitude, both good things.

"Seat belts on. We're about to blast off." Christina cranked the truck as a reserve SUV turned into the parking lot. The immediate spike of nerves annoyed her. This was a park ranger, not a police officer. What could he do, toss her into the tent jail? Feed her to the bears?

Still, when Ash Kingfisher appeared, Christina tried a friendly smile. In this part of the reserve, the one where she lived and worked, he was the ultimate authority.

He had the kind of dark eyes that measured a person and it was impossible not to squirm. "Well, now, that looks like a couple of Hendrixes. Y'all headed in to school?"

"Hi, Ash," Parker said, his clear boyish voice carrying through the parking lot. "Aunt Chris has been staying with us. She's about to make us late for school." He didn't seem all that concerned about it, either.

Ash dipped his head. "Guess Brett will have a few things to tell me when he makes it back into the office."

"Everything is under control, sir." Christina would have slapped her forehead. There was no real reason to call Ash Kingfisher anything other than his name. They hadn't been in the same grade, but they'd gone to school together. The fact that authority seemed woven into his skin was the only explanation. That and the uniform. It was enough to rattle anyone. "We should get going."

He propped his hands on his utility belt. "Drive carefully. Precious cargo and all that."

Christina carefully put the truck in Reverse and slowly rolled out of the parking lot. Mindful of the time, she pressed harder on the accelerator as she headed down the mountain.

"Sir." Riley snorted. "I can't believe you said that."

"Respecting your elders is something you could work on, Riley."

As soon as she heard the words and the bossy tone, Christina checked to see their impact. Neither Riley nor Parker could understand what they were hearing. That was what she'd expected, since she couldn't believe she'd said it.

"Well..." Riley stopped, a confused frown on her face. She had no idea how to argue with such a statement coming from Christina.

For some reason, that tiny wrinkle on Riley's face was the funniest thing Christina had seen in a long, long time. The first giggle that escaped made both kids stare at her as if she was losing her mind. It was a valid concern. Her giggling muscles were rusty and she had to gasp for breath. Luckily, she rolled to a shuddering stop in front of the school in time. "I hope you both have a good day."

Riley was shaking her head as she headed

across the lawn. Parker stopped to wave but spun away as his phone rang. "Dad!" The delighted shriek was easy to hear. Christina waited for them both to disappear inside the school before she hit the gas. If she hurried, she might keep her promise to her boss. Ash Kingfisher's serious face reminded her to ease up on the accelerator. He wasn't a cop, but when she drove inside the reserve, he was part of the law enforcement team and he had a direct line to Brett. Being caught speeding would not go over well, even if his kids were safe and sound at school.

As she parked in front of the campground diner, her phone beeped to announce a text. It was probably Brett. Ever since their awkward conversation where he'd blabbed about his problems and managed to insult her, and then win her sympathy, he'd resorted to texting her for quick updates. His were usually three words. *Everything's on schedule.*

Be home Saturday.

The kids okay?

To be contrary, she'd cut everything back to one-word answers. *Great.*

Great. And *Great.* And if she needed more than one word, she sent multiple texts.

Christina hoped that was driving him nuts.

On her way into the diner, she pulled her phone out of her pocket. The text was from Leanne.

Were you going to tell me about Parker? Should I be worried about Riley, too? If Brett's not there, why didn't you call me? I could have talked to them. I thought I could depend on you.

When she realized she was squeezing the phone hard enough to make her knuckles white, Christina slipped the phone in her pocket and headed into work. She couldn't lose this job.

And she hadn't talked to Leanne because the whole situation was so up in the air. What would she say? Parker was sick, but now he's better. Riley is bitter and deserves to be. Brett is drowning in the storm and his mother is no help.

The truth was that she didn't trust Leanne and that was hard to admit.

At some point, even if she did her best to avoid it, Christina was going to have to tell Leanne how much of a mess she'd left behind.

If she was teetering on the edge of a relapse into addiction, the news could give her a shove over.

Since the breakfast rush was still in full swing, Christina didn't have time to worry about that conversation. Instead, Woody was waving his coffee cup as soon as she stepped inside. Luisa was frazzled because no one should try to cover that many tables on their own. In the same spot, Christina would have been mad. Instead, Luisa said, "Everything okay?"

The unexpected concern surprised Christina. She rubbed stinging eyes and nodded. "It's a lot, taking care of kids by yourself." Her own honesty surprised her, too. That said something about the worry that was seeping in around the edges.

But all she could do was the best that she could. Just like she'd told Riley the night she'd confessed she wasn't enough, and

Woody that morning. Until they'd walked in a person's shoes, who had a right to make judgments?

"You said it, sister, but we stick together, okay? I did it for a long time, until Rodney came along, so I know. You're doing good work," Luisa said as she wiped a hand over her forehead. "You got the corner booth?"

"Yep. All set." Determined to prove her worth as an indifferent but in-need-of-money waitress, Christina hustled around the tables, refilling and clearing as she went. Until the second-to-last customer left, she had no time to think. It was nice.

But Woody was determined to wait until she could talk.

"Whew, that was a busy morning, huh?" He fiddled with the check she'd deposited under the coffee cup half an hour earlier. "Them kids… You're doing a nice thing."

Exhausted, Christina leaned against the counter and fought the urge to move him along. He was a good customer. He'd offered to back her up in a tough situation. Whatever he had to say, she could listen.

Then she realized what he'd said. His praise was unexpected. So much better than a comment on how pretty she was that day. A good thing. Christina straightened.

"I hope you're being real careful." He reached into his back pocket to pull out his wallet. "Word around town is that Brett's half a second from proposing. Guy needs some proper help with those kids. Hate for you to get hurt when he shoves you right back out the door if Leanne ever returns." He handed her a twenty. "You go ahead and keep that change. You did a good deed."

Content with his pronouncement and own good deed, Woody beamed with satisfaction.

After the instant anger that boiled up over Woody's assumption that Brett might come to his senses someday eased, Christina rubbed the bill between her fingers as she decided what to do with his unsolicited advice. Since she knew he was only repeating what he'd heard around Smoky Joe's, Christina could understand where he was coming from.

When Brett got home and found out his kids were being run through the gossip mill, he'd lose his cool. If she wanted to maintain this connection, which was only in place now because of his complete desperation, she owed it to herself to address the rumors. "There's no telling what the story is, Woody, but you and I are friends, right?" She waited for the old guy to nod. "And I expect you to tell the truth whenever you can." He tipped his chin up. "Brett asked me for help. I gave it. I will always give it. I love those kids like they're my own family because they are."

Woody pursed his lips. Before he could say anything about Leanne and all her mistakes, Christina leaned over to squeeze his hand. She didn't want to listen to it. "You understand how family works, don't you?"

"I do." He sighed. "Wife and I never did have kids, but I do like to see my brother's children on the Facebook." He shook his head. "Thank heavens for modern technology. Otherwise, I'd just be an old man, no one to remember me."

Hearing him say the fear that might have kept her up more than once made it necessary to stand tall. "Don't you get taken advantage of, though. He ain't for you. Leanne done proved that. I guess he says he'll marry you because of love or something, but maybe he's using you as a stand-in."

Christina's mouth dropped open and shock froze her feet to the floor. Marry her? No way. Then she realized that was the story making the rounds in Sweetwater. How could anyone believe that was the truth? Had they said it as a joke and laughed in disbelief? She wanted to argue, to shut down the whole thing immediately, or at least point out the serious flaws in the story, but the fact that it would solve all of her problems and most of Brett's made it difficult to give in to the ridiculousness of it all.

She was shaking her head slowly as she cleared Woody's plate. His cheerful goodbye barely registered as she stared down at the stack of dirty dishes.

"You okay over there?" Luisa called as she counted out the tips from the jar to split with Monroe. "Getting two kids to school always made me crazy."

Christina cleared her throat. "Sure. Fine." She pulled Woody's twenty out of her pocket. "I need to ring this up, and then pay for Riley and Parker."

Another dip into the tiny pool of money

she'd made. At this rate, she'd end up owing more than just the sum to Janet Abernathy.

The reminder of the woman she'd run into in the grocery store stopped Christina in her tracks. Was that where the rumor had started?

She did her best to replay the conversation in her mind. If it was, Brett was going to imagine seven different ways to murder her and hide her body. He'd never follow through, but in the same spot, Christina would be creative herself.

"You heard any rumors about Brett Hendrix getting remarried?" Christina asked Luisa as she made change.

"Well, now…" Luisa didn't look up from the simple task of counting out three pennies. "I'll say it didn't shock me when you walked in with his kids this morning."

Christina's knees folded and she flopped down on a stool. "Oh no. This could be a problem."

What if Brett thought she'd started the rumor in order to… Do what? For what possible reason would she have encouraged the town to think there was anything between them but antagonism and a whole lot of history? The urge to argue, to explain what had happened was so strong that the words got caught in her throat. Panic shot her pulse rate up and Christina desperately wanted something to drink.

He'd warned her against using this opportunity to reunite Leanne with her kids when the idea had never occurred to her. What sort of scheming would he accuse her of now?

He'd grown up here, too. Brett Hendrix understood how gossip made the rounds in this town. He'd ignore it.

Wouldn't he?

Then there was Leanne. What would her best friend think if she heard the story? Would she brush it off because she understood Christina had her back in all things?

That morning's text suggested that history was losing some of its power.

Leanne would come back to town to fight for Brett and her kids. Then Christina could explain the misunderstanding and everyone would agree it was a silly story. They might laugh about it.

Everyone but Brett.

At this point, there was no stopping the

town's grapevine. All she could do was manage the fallout. The only question was would Brett or Leanne be the first to explode?

CHAPTER EIGHT

SPENDING A WEEK away from his kids had never been something Brett enjoyed. Even when he'd been a kid himself, he'd loved every minute he'd had to hold Riley in his arms. The thing about being the father of the prettiest baby girl in the entire world was that it was so easy to fall head over heels in love, even as she derailed every plan Brett ever made. He'd never intended to be married and the father of one at nineteen, but when he'd stopped fighting and made up his mind to do the right thing, he'd found the first part of his calling.

Police work had been the second part. A man needed a career. His young wife had never seemed stable enough for him to be gone for long periods of time, so the military was out. Finding the advertisement for the Knoxville Police Department had seemed like a bolt from the blue.

His whole career had started with one scared phone call, and he'd thanked his lucky stars more than once that he'd been goaded into making it.

By the woman who was currently in charge of keeping the only two people who mattered in this entire world safe and sound and in one piece.

As he loaded up his SUV, Brett forced himself not to imagine all the things that might have gone wrong while he was away. They'd played in a solid loop in his head for four days straight.

He'd talked to Parker every day and Riley whenever she would answer his calls. Texts from Christina seemed to indicate she was still alive and not being held hostage in a closet by his angry daughter.

He had nothing to worry about.

After settling into the front seat, he punched in Christina's number and waited for her to answer.

"Yes, we're fine. Yes, the house is still standing. I haven't had any wild parties and the secondary drug-trafficking business I'm running is currently experiencing a slow period. You'll be home tomorrow.

What more could you need to know?" Christina said in lieu of the generally accepted greeting.

"If I didn't know better, I'd demand proof that Riley was my daughter instead of yours. The two of you…" Brett shook his head. "I wanted to let someone know that I'm hitting the road tonight. If I die in a fiery crash somewhere on I-40, tell my kids I loved them."

The beat of silence on the line would have made him think the call had dropped except his vehicle wasn't in motion. Brett squinted into the orange glow of the setting sun while he waited for her answer.

"Okay. I'm sorry." The words were nice, even if they weren't sincere. "It's been a long day. Doing this by myself has been a challenge."

Brett closed his eyes as he fought back the word jumble that wanted to spill from his mouth. So many people told him they admired him, even while there was pity in their eyes, because of all that he was doing. What a relief it was to hear someone else say all the things he was dying to. It was a challenge. Day in and out, he was hanging by a thread.

Christina understood that thread. For all their differences, she got that and it was the most important piece of his life.

"But I don't need to tell you that, do I?" she added softly. "My patience is exhausted, too, Brett, but you're the one who gets it. Your kids are both in their rooms. Parker is watching reruns of his favorite television show, since I refuse to ever let it play in the living room again. And Riley... Well, I'll tell you more about that when you get here." She quickly added, "She's fine. We're all healthy, reasonably happy and safe. There's nothing to worry about. Really."

Brett rolled his head on his shoulders, the crack and pop of tense muscles felt good and made him that much more fatigued at the same time. Almost everyone else there for training was going to leave bright and early in the morning. A smart man would do the same, but he wanted to be home.

"I believe you. I'll be home soon." The words rolled off his tongue easily, almost like he could remember how it had felt to say them and have someone care to hear them. "And I'll owe you big-time."

Christina sighed. "Remember you said that." Her low laugh worried him and sent a weird shiver of…something up his spine. He'd never once imagined her as anything other than a pain in the neck.

But it was so easy to picture her smile, small but genuine. If she was as tired as she sounded, her eyes might show it, but how amazing would it be to see the real Christina, the one hidden under the hard shell?

As a kid, he'd thought he owed it to his wife to help Christina, to save Leanne's best friend from the wild road she'd been on.

The older he got, the clearer it became that she'd been the one pulling herself and Leanne through life. Now she'd stepped up alongside him to shoulder some of the weight he carried. It was impossible not to admire that fearlessness and heart. Whatever the right words were for someone who jumped in feetfirst to work hard because someone she loved needed assistance, they described Christina.

He knew it was rare enough to treasure it when he found it.

"I won't forget that you saved me," Brett said, and then repeated it. He wouldn't. And if he was the man he wanted to be, he'd make a change now that he knew the truth. What would that look like? Regular visits with Parker and Riley, definitely.

"Be safe on the road." She ended the call before he could respond. As Brett tossed his phone on the passenger seat, the weird sadness that settled over him was a surprise. He hadn't been ready to say goodbye.

Which was going to be a problem, if he let it.

Christina might have shown him strength that he hadn't expected.

Admiring that was one thing.

Falling for it? That would lead to a whole lot of heartache.

Brett reversed out of the parking spot and left the motel without a backward glance.

How far was he prepared to go to help Christina? And would he be able to lean on her until he had a new plan? He'd been working on finding a new, easygoing, good woman to marry. All he wanted was a stable family life.

Leanne had been all about the highs of passion and new love and the lows of disappointment and the dangers of an obsessive personality.

He'd found his callings: dad and cop. As a husband, he'd done his best, and with the right woman, he could make it work.

The drive back to Sweetwater was easy and long enough to give him plenty of time to think.

Unfortunately, as he pulled down his driveway close to midnight, he had exactly zero answers on where to find the mother for his kids or how best to help Christina.

Worn from the constant thinking and the strain of driving the dark roads in the mountains, Brett considered sleeping in the front seat of the SUV. The walk to the front door seemed too long.

Then he remembered he was a grown man with a nice, comfortable bed inside and so left the SUV. Lugging his duffel out of the back was equivalent to lifting a train, but he trudged up the steps to his front door and enjoyed the peace that always settled over him as he listened to the croak of frogs and a slight breeze in the trees.

Nashville had nice restaurants and enough excitement to keep a man busy for days, but he'd never miss it.

Home would always be this peaceful feeling.

He quietly unlocked the front door, pleased to see that it was secure. The night he'd come home from a late shift to find that his mother had gone to bed without locking the door had been one of the longest he'd ever spent. That had been enough to make him wonder if he could trust her to keep his kids safe.

At least Christina had passed that test.

Brett set his duffel down with a relieved sigh and straightened as the lights blazed and Christina stepped around the corner of the hall with her arms raised, a bat gripped in both hands.

Their eyes locked.

"Lower your weapon." Brett held up both hands. "Killer."

Christina immediately lowered her arms, the motion jerky. "Sorry. I've never heard anyone except people with bad intentions move that quietly." She propped the bat on the wall and yanked her T-shirt down over her hips. "Welcome home."

At almost any other point of the day, he'd process things more quickly, but Brett blinked slowly as he worked through what he wanted to say. "You were prepared to bash an intruder over the head. Why aren't you sleeping?" He had so many questions. Was that the most important one? No, but it had to have the least upsetting answer.

"I never sleep too soundly." Christina pointed at the nest of blankets on the couch. "And I was right there. First line of defense." Her small smile suggested she was attempting a joke. At midnight. After she'd come ready to face off against an intruder. Her swift change of direction reminded him a bit of his ex-wife's. They were both so smart, alert, ready to face whatever came along.

Instead of hunting for the next adventure, though, Christina was hunkered down, prepared to defend herself and his kids against…what?

"Have a lot of late-night, unexpected, unwanted visitors?" Brett asked as he eased around her into his living room. The warm glow of the table lamp had been enough to light up the room until Christina's security defense. Did she sleep with the light on because it was an unfamiliar house?

"Not as many as you think, I'm sure." Christina shrugged as if it didn't matter what he thought. "But it doesn't hurt to be prepared."

Brett had never had to "be prepared" for something like that. He'd grown up in a comfy house with two parents who cared even if they'd been too busy to parent. After his dad died, his mother had hit the road for far-flung adventures. Since he'd been knee-deep in broken toys and diapers by that point, it had been easy enough to let her be responsible for her own safety.

Was this how Leanne and Christina had grown up?

"You don't have to look at me like a bug in a jar, Officer." Christina rolled her eyes. "That cabin, in the middle of nowhere… I have to think things through. After Diane left, I borrowed one of Parker's bats and propped it in the corner. It's no big deal. I knew you'd hunt me to the ends of the earth if anything happened to the kids. I was thinking ahead." Her dry voice might convince him she meant what she said, but she didn't meet his eyes. "You thought I was incapable of planning, but I'm not."

She folded her legs under her as she sat in the middle of the couch. "Now, I need my beauty sleep. I'll be up and on my way into the campground before y'all get up in the morning."

She was up late and would be back at work before the sun rose.

"Luisa will be glad I don't have to make the school run in the middle of the breakfast rush," Christina said through a wide yawn.

She was lucky she hadn't lost her job. He'd done whatever he needed to keep his while she'd put hers on the line. For him.

Brett rubbed his forehead at the realization of how much he owed Christina.

"I'll call you tomorrow," he said as he watched her slide slowly down the couch, her second yawn convincing him it was time to move on. "I want to talk to you about…things. Like a job."

Her eyes popped open. "A job? Could

I work it around shifts at the diner?" She leaned on an elbow, and then shook her head. "Oh, you mean babysitting. Sure. That's not a job. That's a favor." She drew the word out slowly as if he might have trouble understanding her. Her resemblance to Riley in that second was scary.

"No, a *job*. With money and possibly transportation." His truck was no fancy ride, but it did have four wheels and an engine. "Yes, you could work at the diner. Meet the kids at the bus stop, figure out dinner." Laundry, grocery shopping... Was he looking for a housekeeper more than a wife? "I want someone here that Riley will talk to, so..."

She shook her head. "Doesn't matter. That smells like charity. I don't take it." Her firm jaw supported her claim.

Brett raised both hands. "It's too late to argue. I want to kiss Parker good-night and hover in Riley's doorway until she moves like she senses I'm there. Then I will duck out and get some sleep so that I can go talk to my boss about why I can never do this again, at least not until I find them a step-mother or something." Why was it every time he said that out loud, he liked the plan less? It was good, solid.

For him and his family. What woman would benefit from the arrangement?

Too tired to stand his growing doubt, Brett would have made his escape except Christina held up one finger. "About that."

This was it, whatever she hadn't wanted to tell him, she was about to lay on him, robbing him of his slowly growing peace and any sleep he might get.

"There's a story making the rounds in town." Christina grimaced. "You aren't going to like it."

Brett tried counting to whatever number it was that would make it easy to swallow the lump in his throat. "Let me guess. Leanne ran away because of something I did." That would be easy enough to handle. It was partially true. He would let it ride.

Christina blinked slowly. "Brett, you're always the hero in the town of Sweetwater. No one would dare accuse you of that, not when Leanne Fisker is around." Her bitter smile was more familiar. "For better or worse, you'll get a pass from Sweetwater."

Brett moved to sit next to her, too tired

to stand. He hated being the subject of the coffee talk at Smoky Joe's, but he was the one who'd stayed, who was raising his kids.

"Well, hit me with it, then." He did his best to brace for impact and put his feet up on the coffee table as she leaned back. Christina's shoulder brushed his and the clean scent of shampoo and laundry detergent made him smile.

"Janet Abernathy thinks we're engaged, so now the rest of the town does, too." She gasped at the end as if she'd lost her breath in the hurry to get it all out.

Brett frowned as he processed that information. "That has nothing to do with Riley. I thought it would be about Riley." Why was his brain moving so slowly? What did it matter what he'd thought before she laid her bombshell on him? The two of them engaged?

"Oh, I talked her out of dyeing her hair blue. I'm not sure that was the right thing to do because it's just hair and every kid goes through phases like that. She told me her best friend, Naya, had done it and I almost agreed, but then I pictured you blasting off like a bottle rocket and told her to wait until you got home." Christina stopped talking to peer cautiously at him. His whole life, he'd never once seen her look so carefully concerned.

Why wouldn't his brain work? Was this what a stroke felt like? The world kept turning, but he was hung up on a single second, the one where *engaged* left Christina's mouth.

The fact that it immediately seemed like everything turned crystal clear had to be a trick of whatever breakdown of logic and reason he was experiencing.

"I'm sorry. You're mad. I knew you would be. It was an honest mistake. I ran into her while I was buying Parker's medicine, and something I said gave her that idea. I was going to straighten her out when I went in to pay her back for the groceries I couldn't afford, but by the time I found out, I figured the damage was already done. And I still have to pay her back." Christina slapped her hands on the cushions. "I should go home tonight. I'll take the truck and return it after my shift at the Branch." She stood and paced around the room. "As soon as I figure out where my shoes are."

Over the years, he'd learned a few of Christina's expressions. The one he knew the best was bitter anger. In the middle of the night, confused over where her shoes might have disappeared to, she was only a beautiful, tired woman who needed to be sleeping instead of talking. He intercepted her in the middle of a march into the dining room. He held out a hand and she stopped. He tugged gently to urge her back to the couch. "Sit. Please. I don't have the energy to watch you pace."

Her disgruntled laugh was as charming as her crazy bed hair.

"I honestly don't know how you do this, Brett." She shook her head. "After one week, I'm tired, I started a dumb story through the rumor mill and somehow my shoes have gone." Then she brightened. "I remember. I picked everything up off the floor and put the stuff that should be hanging in the closet *in the closet*. Somehow, the pile in front of the door grows every time I turn my back. All the shoes are in the bottom." She moved to check, but Brett wrapped his hand loosely around her arm.

"Christina, stop." Whatever it was that

usually irritated him about her was missing there in the middle of the night. She wasn't a seductress on the move in that moment or even a brittle warrior. She was totally human. Tired, scattered and annoyed with him.

She'd never been more attractive.

Brett waited for her to settle again, relieved when she went quietly.

"If you're about to accuse me of scheming my way in or trying to catch you somehow, just don't." Her shoulders slumped. "When the story makes it back to Leanne, she'll take care of that for you. I wouldn't have told you, but I knew you'd hear about it and…" She sighed. "I want to help."

As she eased down into the cushions beside him, she bumped into him, and he remembered his wish to have someone who cared whether he made it home. Brett wouldn't have named Christina as an option if anyone had asked him who he might marry, but there, in the middle of the night, with no anger between them and Leanne a shadow on the outside, it made more sense than he expected. Christina loved Parker and Riley. They would be an incentive for her.

He rested his head against her shoulder, mainly to keep her in place, but he was relieved when she tipped her own head to rest against his. Like they did this all the time, shared the troubles of the day.

After a peaceful minute where her breathing slowed, Brett leaned back.

"I'm not going to accuse you of anything. If I ever do that again, remind me that I promised not to be a self-righteous jerk ever again." Her eyes widened. Christina didn't believe him, and he understood her doubts, but he didn't want to be that guy ever again, so he doubled down. "I mean it. If I slip, call me on it. Remind me that I said this. Every day I've been away from home, I've remembered how rigid I've been. Not the same incident over and over, but separate occasions when I could have been easier, nicer, more helpful to you. It's… I'm ashamed. I know better." That string of words hurt. Brett paused to consider the pain. "I see it better now, Chris."

"You're not mad that I'm dragging you

through the gossip rounds again?" Christina asked slowly.

Oh yeah, the part he hated. "I don't love it." Brett sighed. "It hurts the kids."

"I get that." She shrugged. "Who in their right minds would believe such a story anyway? That's the part I don't get. This town has seen enough of both of us to know we don't belong together."

Brett scratched his chin. He wasn't sure how to answer that.

"Where's my agreement? Those people are willfully ignoring reality at this point. They're repeating the story because they want to…scoff or laugh or something." She leaned closer to study his face. "Right?"

More than anything he wanted to reassure her. Where had that come from? It was the hour. That had to be it. He couldn't summon up enough energy to jump on the bandwagon. The fact that the suggestion didn't shock him as much as it had Christina was something he needed to think about after he got plenty of sleep.

"Thank you for keeping my kids safe, Chris." He decided to take a chance and wrapped an arm around her shoulders to squeeze her closer. Growing up, she'd always smelled of hair spray and drugstore perfume. Not tonight. Tonight was the exact opposite.

Christina blinked. "Wow. I didn't think you could surprise me, but tonight you've done it."

Because he'd been so rigid.

She was right. Something was changing inside him, probably thanks to unrelenting pressure and the lack of any other options. If she knew that two urges were battling for control inside him, she'd be shocked. He was either going to kiss her or run for cover. There, in the warm glow of home and being connected, it seemed the most natural thing in the world to press his lips to hers. What would she do? "I'm loosening up."

Her head drew back. "No way."

Brett laughed. "Get some rest. Come back here after your shift. We'll talk then." *Move in. Help me help Riley. Give me a chance to breathe.*

Save me.

That was what it all boiled down to. He

was half a second from…what? How far would he go to have help?

"What do we have to talk about?" she asked. "Schedules and plans and…what? You could text me when you need me to pick up the kids or…whatever."

What was he doing? Was he considering the strangest suggestion of all? Marriage to Christina was nowhere on the list of ideas he'd examined and discarded on the drive home.

Sitting there next to her, talking about his life, it didn't seem so strange anymore.

For some reason, this version of his future seemed right. She could work less, enjoy more. If there was anyone on this earth who might have the patience to understand his thirteen-year-old girl, it was Christina.

But what would Christina get out of the relationship? A nice place to stay, a rattletrap truck and daily connection to the kids she loved. There was no way that would be enough for her.

There was only one thing that mattered to Christina that he could offer.

"Come to dinner. We'll talk about what to do for Leanne."

Watching her mouth snap shut in surprise was satisfying. "Okay."

"Okay. I'm going to go hug my daughter." Nothing else mattered at that point. Parker and Riley were okay. He had time to think about Christina and Leanne and what made the most sense for everyone. He could do this.

For the first time in a long time, he believed that deeply. Life would go on. He and Parker and Riley would make it through this. He could find the answer.

And if he could find a solution they both approved of, Christina could be part of that answer.

CHAPTER NINE

WAKING UP ON the couch at Brett Hendrix's cozy house had become an easy thing to enjoy. The golden light of the table lamp showed cheery clutter that she'd battled for the first day before surrendering to the inevitable. The parents of two active kids must learn early which battles they can win. Wasting precious energy on something she'd never accomplish had never been her style.

Determined to be the best houseguest Brett had never imagined, Christina folded the blankets she'd claimed from the hall linen closet on the first night. Washing them would be even better, but not at this hour of the morning. If she decided to show up for dinner, she could ambush the washing machine and have them sudsing before Brett knew what hit him. She tiptoed into the kitchen and started the precious coffee.

He'd never notice the single cup she poured into the mug she'd been using.

"Good morning." Brett stood in the kitchen doorway, one hand braced against it as if he needed the support. "Or is this hour still considered night?"

Since she'd had similar thoughts on the mornings she'd trudged up the mountain to the diner, Christina could sympathize. "Definitely night. Why are you awake?" Christina wasn't certain that he was awake. Maybe he was a sleepwalker. Was she still asleep, too? Their hushed voices, the stillness of the morning and the shadowy kitchen could have been a dream.

She watched him pour a cup of coffee and lift it to his nose to inhale deeply. His eyes opened. Was sleep coffee drinking a thing? Maybe he was the first case.

"I'm going to take the kids out on the lake today. Good fishing starts early." He sighed. "Why did I agree to do that? I have the day off. I could be napping."

"Must be because you're a good dad." Christina scooted the coffee mug he sat on the edge of the counter toward safety. "Still seems early."

He leaned his hip against the counter and scrubbed his hand through his hair. If he was hot in an authoritative way in full uniform and ranger hat, he was irresistible in the early morning in a faded T-shirt and sweatpants. Almost.

The urge to brush her hand against soft cotton on the way to pressing a kiss to his lips was upsetting.

And so strong.

"I have to get to work." Christina moved toward the door as he wrapped his hand around her arm.

"Don't forget your coffee." He pointed at the cup as his hand slid slowly away, the warmth fading as he stepped back. "I'll stop in with the kids to grab some pie later." He cleared his throat. "If that's okay."

Confused, Christina grabbed the mug, and then let go as hot coffee spilled down the side. "I've got a short shift today. Just breakfast. I'm not sure I'll still be there."

Brett nodded and Christina picked up the mug again.

"You could come out with us. To the lake. To fish." He wiped up the spill without a pause. Fatherhood had given him skills. "Do you fish?"

He'd forgotten the first time they fished together. That was enough of a reminder of who she was to him that it should help her step back. Why wasn't it working? Now she wanted a kiss and a day out on the lake where she could torment him for forgetting the romantic excursion Leanne had planned. He'd completely torpedoed it by insisting Christina come along. Leanne's revenge had been swift and involved lots of whining.

"Riley just sits in the boat. You could do that. If you wanted to." Brett cleared his throat again. Was he nervous? That made two of them. "I'll ask you later. Maybe you'll be too tired. Short day would mean plenty of time for a nice nap." He seemed so wistful when he said it, like naps were dreams that never came true.

"Why are you awake?" she asked again. It made no sense. There was no way he'd rouse Parker up for hours.

"I wanted to make sure I had a chance to tell you to have a good day." One corner of his mouth curled up. "Sweet, right?"

Since it had never happened to her in her life before that minute, Christina wasn't sure what to call it.

"Someone to wait up for. Someone to kiss as they walk out the door." He shook his head. "That's the kind of thing I want, you know? It's nice to be cared for."

"Well, sure, but…" Being speechless was new and scary. She might not always speak her mind, but she was never without opinions. This whole conversation was so strange that her brain would no longer compute.

"You're going to be later than usual." Brett topped off her coffee. "Have a good day at work. We'll see you later."

On her way out the door, Christina turned off the light, hid the bat inside the coat closet and took a careful look to make sure she wasn't leaving anything valuable.

Because it was time to put some distance between her and Brett. The whole morning conversation made her feel restless and anxious and excited about the day. What was going on with him?

He'd accepted her major mistake easily enough at midnight. When he had enough time to get a good mad on, he'd rescind his invitation. There would be yelling. Reasonable Brett had a way of morphing into uptight, self-righteous Brett when he had time to think.

But he'd ordered her not to let him slip back into that. The more he let that side go, the better she liked him. They could work a real arrangement out.

And then there was his offer to talk about how to help Leanne. She had to be desperately missing her kids. Since Christina had never answered her last text, she was also angry.

The night before, Christina had done her best to soak up every precious second with Riley and Parker before they disappeared inside their rooms. She'd taken a selfie with each of them because they'd refused to be in the same shot. Refereeing their bickering had taken some practice, but Christina was getting better.

It was almost like being a part of a family.

Or what she imagined that would be like. Squabbling over dinner and dishes and television, yes, but a slowly building history that no one else would understand.

Being on the inside could be addictive.

"Get a grip, girl." Opening the front door reminded her of how much ground there was still to gain. "You don't have any choice but to take that truck. Get to it."

It was too easy. Easy things were dangerous. Falling in love with being with Riley and Parker was going to hurt her. Depending on Brett for anything would make it hurt worse. Trusting him could lead to falling for him. Was that even possible? She needed some distance.

Before she turned the key in the ignition, Christina pulled out her phone and scrolled through her contacts for any other option for a ride to work. Leaving the truck would be a good message for Brett. He'd understand she wasn't taking anything from him.

Was Woody the kind of friend who wouldn't mind getting a call at this time of the morning? Better question, was his wife the kind of woman who accepted that her husband answered cries for help before sunrise?

"Better take the truck." Christina started it and pulled away down the street. At the stop sign, she stared hard in the rearview mirror. Why did homesickness feel so awful? And it wasn't even her home. She had a perfectly acceptable cabin. It was actually *hers*.

But she never felt this sadness and a touch of nerves as she drove away from it.

Maneuvering through the mountains was easy enough. Rays were outlining the peaks when she parked in front of the campground diner.

Woody was sitting on a bench next to the door.

"Thought I'd get me an early start this morning. Fish will be biting." Woody held the door open for her and Christina waved at Luisa as she tied on her apron. "I'll have me the usual."

The usual? No staring at the menu thoughtfully while he pretended not to be a creature of habit. Things were looking up.

"You know what that is?" Woody asked, concern wrinkling his brow.

"Let me surprise you." Christina scribbled the order down and passed it through the window before she poured his coffee.

"Brett back in town?" Woody asked as he blew on the hot coffee to cool it. His first slurp resulted in a happy sigh. As it always did.

For some reason, the sameness of the morning routine didn't bother her as much as usual. Maybe she was getting the hang of waiting tables. Finally. A full decade of jobs like it ought to come with some perks soon.

"Why do you ask?" Christina stared out at the misty lake and wondered how nice it might be to have one day to sit on a shore somewhere. She could dangle her feet in the water, listen to the birds and ignore the snapping finger of the jerk in the corner who was ready to order.

"No kids. Figured he must be back. No way his mama came home. That woman was desperate to brush the dust of this town away." Woody pointed. "I could take you out. That look tells me Otter Lake is calling to you. I heard that call often enough."

When Monroe mumbled, "Order up," Christina hustled over to get Woody's breakfast. The old guy's pleased surprise tickled her. She'd gotten so comfortable being annoyed at his insistence on pretending he wasn't the same every day that the pleasure of watching his excitement that she'd remembered him and his order was sweet. If she put in a bit more effort, how much satisfaction could she get in return?

The guy with the snapping fingers added a craned neck and she remembered why it would never do to get her hopes up.

"I might take you up on that. Next day off I get, take me to your best fishing hole." Christina laughed at his suspicious glare. "Or your worst one. I won't know the difference."

He waved his finger at her before diving into his breakfast, and Christina turned up the charm for the impatient guy in the corner. For most of the morning, she was busy enough to ignore the way the locals came in, watched her, talked about her and immediately clammed up when she turned in their direction.

She should be used to it by now.

Then reserve ranger Brett Hendrix stepped inside and all conversation in the diner stopped. Even in his weekend casual jeans and flannel, Brett was strong and tall, the authority he wore so easily a permanent fixture.

When Brett wore his uniform, his freshly

shaven jawline and gleaming shoes a part of the requirements, he presented the wholesome image of truth and justice. It was easy to imagine him cradling a baby in one arm while he assisted an elderly woman across a busy intersection, the flag billowing out behind him like a cape. But like this? Dressed for a day on the lake, unshaven and comfortable. This was a man who would be easy to live with. He would be easy to love.

If she'd been a different person, Christina would admit that there was not another man in Sweetwater who matched Brett Hendrix for appeal.

And that was an inconvenient realization, since he was her best friend's ex.

Brett surveyed the crowd, doing his best to determine what he'd interrupted, before turning to her. The question in his eyes was easy to read but impossible to answer, so she pulled out her order pad. "What can I get you, Officer?"

His lips tightened at the title she trotted out when she wanted to irritate him.

Why did she want to irritate him that morning? Christina promised herself she'd figure out the answer later.

"Three pieces of pie to go. Unless I can convince you to join us." No sound went through the diner, but something changed in the air. Brett glanced over his shoulder again before giving her a "can you believe the nerve?" look. The number of people eavesdropping was hard to ignore.

"Oh, can't leave. The place is swamped." Christina waved a hand in the general direction of the manager's office. "Luisa needs me." She hurried to bag up the pie, but Denise, the waitress taking over the lunch shift, shimmied between her and the counter before she finished.

"Sorry I'm late, girl. You go ahead." Denise was already moving between the tables with a pot of coffee before Christina could find a way out.

When she turned back to Brett, he was watching her closely. "Please come, Christina." It was impossible to look away from his eyes. Over the years, she'd seen plenty of different emotions there. This time, she could read an honest request and possibly a little bit of amusement at her predicament.

"Don't forget your pie," Luisa said as she pushed a fourth to-go container across the counter. "Beautiful day to be out on the lake. Enjoy it."

"Don't rightly know if they's bitin' over at the falls, but it sure is a pretty scene." Woody waggled his eyebrows. "Real romantic-like."

So she had no help. Even Woody was ready to shove her into Brett's arms.

"Parker likes to yell to listen to the echoes. Not sure that's the mood we'll get, but I'll take it under consideration." Brett waved the bag. "Are you ready?"

No, she wasn't. Christina glanced over Brett's shoulder to see Riley leaning out the passenger window of the reserve SUV. Once she caught Christina's eye, she made the "would you hurry up?" motion as only an aggravated teen girl can. A long streak of blue hair dangled over her shoulder.

Brett turned back. "Don't send me out all alone with her."

Christina laughed. This Brett was almost irresistible. When his kids got in on the conversation, she was unable to say no. "I see she talked you into letting her go blue."

"As a wise woman once said, it's only hair." He rubbed his hand down his nape. "It made her happy. How is a father supposed to fight that?" Then he grimaced and said in what was no doubt supposed to be a teenage girl tone, "But, Da-a-d, everyone in school has already colored their hair. I'm the only weird one."

He widened his eyes at her.

"You've had a busy morning." When she'd left at the crack of dawn, Brett had been half-awake and Riley's hair had been brown.

"They catch me when I'm at my weakest." He clasped his hands together. "Don't send me out alone with them."

Christina's lips twitched as she weighed her choices one last time. "Defend me, protect me, please."

"Ash's fishing boat will seat us all comfortably. We've got a cooler filled with drinks and almost zero chance of catching anything because Riley has a fishing playlist that she will bless us all with. Even if we do catch anything, she will force us to toss it back because of animal rights or something like that. Parker will complain about…something, when he's not shouting excitedly about everything else. It'll be fun." Brett braced a hand against the diner door and shoved it open. "Just watch where you cast. I don't want a hook in my nose."

Woody's cackle faded as they stepped out into the parking lot. Before they made it to the SUV, Christina said, "Why are you doing this? Really. I'll help. This seems… unlike you."

Brett lowered his head and studied the faded lines on the asphalt. "Yeah. It does, but I don't want it to."

She wanted to demand that he explain himself, but Parker hit the horn. "Let's go. Fish are waiting."

Christina studied the clear blue sky. It was a beautiful October day that she'd spend sleeping and doing laundry if she didn't seize her chance.

Brett tugged a ball cap out of his back pocket and slipped it on. Then he grinned and all the worries and the years and bad history dropped away. Lake bum suited him. In the sunshine, the scruff on his jaw showed a hint of silver here and there. And the happy grin was that of a man truly content with every bit of his life. In that moment, in the bright sunshine of the campground parking lot, he was irresistible.

"Have you got another hat like that for me?" Christina asked as she took the bag holding their dessert from him.

"Only one lucky fishing hat in the world," Brett drawled, "but if you're in trouble, I'll loan it to you."

"That's a generous offer," she said as she put her hand on the SUV's door. "Should I be suspicious?"

Brett took his hat off, and then set it easily over her ponytail. "Nah. It's easy to be generous with a pretty girl on a perfect October weekend." Then he clapped one hand on the hood. "Don't catch more fish than I do or there will be trouble."

"So fragile." Christina was shaking her head as she climbed in the front seat. She could make herself sick worrying over what was going on with Brett, or she could enjoy the afternoon. Since the opportunity would never come around again, she decided to go with it.

And that meant she was determined to catch more fish than Brett.

Before he started the car, he leaned forward to say, "I haven't forgotten my promise to help." He waited for her to meet his stare, and then nodded. He was talking about Leanne without saying her name. "Monday. I'm on the case on Monday. When I go into work, I'll see what I can find out."

Sobered at the reminder that her best friend was out there in the world and she might be in trouble, Christina started to protest. If he could do it Monday, why couldn't he do it today? She had time. She could go.

"Dad, I've been waiting forever," Parker yelled from the back seat. "Let's get out on the water."

"Time with my kids. That's what I'm doing today." He waited for her to nod, squeezed her arm, and then started the SUV. "Bets on how many fish we'll catch? Parker?"

Christina rolled down the window and enjoyed the cool breeze that loosened her ponytail. He was right. She could take an afternoon off. Putting the rest of the world on hold to enjoy a few hours would make the next step less grueling. And he'd made her a promise. On Monday, Brett Hendrix would help her track down Leanne.

Then they could figure out what came next in their lives.

Until then, she was a Hendrix from the inside. She could enjoy it while it lasted.

CHAPTER TEN

INVITING CHRISTINA TO join them had been one thing. Brett could blame that on the early hour and the weird closeness he'd felt staring at her over morning coffee. Following her to work and convincing her to go along in the family ride was a whole different level of crazy.

Why had he persisted? At her first no, he could have easily bowed out, but seeing her there, surrounded by all the curious faces, and knowing how hard she worked at the diner and had taken care of his kids and… He couldn't walk away. The old Brett would have left her there alone, because he was determined to protect his family first.

If anyone deserved a beautiful afternoon on one of the prettiest lakes in East Tennessee, it was hardworking Christina Braswell. The concerned citizens of Sweetwater could take their interest and…

"This is the life," Christina murmured as she leaned over the edge of the boat to trail her fingers through the water. "Why don't we do this every day?"

The full-steam irritation building as he considered how many bad decisions he'd made in order to appease the people who might judge him disappeared in a puff of her happy sigh.

If it hadn't worked out beautifully, he might regret the impulse that had convinced him to turn into the campground parking lot. Riley's uncharacteristic giggles at the way Christina squealed when she dangled her feet over the side of the boat near the falls had driven apart the tiny crack that had been growing ever since she'd answered his SOS.

Then Parker had dared her to bait her own hook with one of the worms he'd been too squeamish to touch himself. When she'd done it flawlessly before tossing the line out to reel in the biggest catch of the day, his son's jaw had dropped.

Brett understood why. If Leanne had been there, her complaining would have already driven them off the water. Too much sitting still and bugs and nature all around.

But Christina? Her ponytail was crooked. Her shirt had wet splotches here and there, which should not be inspected too closely.

And her nose was turning the prettiest shade of pink.

He pulled off his lucky hat and tugged it down over her forehead.

"What's this for? I don't think I'm the one who needs luck." Christina motioned over her shoulder at the cooler. "I've got dinner covered. Well, I've got *my* dinner covered."

Riley straightened in her seat. "You've been keeping them?" Her horrified tone was familiar. So was the wild way she shook her head. She'd inherited Leanne's drama. "No. No, no. No." She moved to the cooler and yanked open the lid. "Back in the water." She pointed so imperiously, it did not invite discussion, so he and Christina knelt in the bottom of the boat to rescue the three healthy fish swimming in the cold water of the cooler.

After they were nothing but a memory and a faint glint of jaunty tail splashes, Christina frowned. "I had my dinner covered." Then she wrinkled her nose. "I like catching them. I don't like cleaning them. I guess it's all for the best, even if I am the world's greatest fisherman." She rinsed her hands again over the side of the boat, wiped them on her shirt and resumed her spot. Instead of picking up her pole, she leaned back on her elbows and tilted her face to the sun.

"Beginner's luck," Brett murmured as he tugged the hat down lower. "But that won't save you from a sunburn."

Christina scoffed, but she didn't take off the hat. "This isn't my first time. This isn't even the first time I've fished with you. You remember our senior year? Leanne had a romantic picnic planned where she'd reveal…" She glanced at Riley, who was bopping her head along with whatever song was coming from her phone. Parker was bopping alongside, thanks to the sharing of the earbuds.

He wanted to believe a day out on the lake had revolutionized his children's relationship and ability to get along. Most likely, it was boredom. And only short-lived.

"But you insisted on bringing me along." Christina pointed a finger at him.

Brett stared out over the lake as he tried to remember that day. "Now that you mention it, I can sort of remember. Was she wearing heels? On the boat?" Christina's nod and laugh made it easier to look back on that day with a smile. If he recalled, after he'd dropped Christina off at her trailer, Leanne had told him Riley was on the way. The flood of panic and grief over everything he was losing had wiped away a pretty funny memory.

It had taken him weeks to come to terms with the changes he had to make and a split second to fall in love with his new baby girl.

"I was, too. Her grandmother picked those shoes up for us at a thrift store in Knoxville and we didn't take them off the whole summer. We also didn't let silly things like practicality rob us of our beauty then." Christina fluffed her tangled hair. "My, how the mighty have fallen, am I right?"

Her naked feet wiggled in the sunshine.

"You've gotten so much wiser in your advanced years." Brett dodged the lazy smack she aimed in his direction and noted how easy it was to be with her. "And right now, you're so pretty it hurts to look at you."

"Right." Christina opened one eye, her suspicion clear. "I smell like fish, Brett."

His chuckle caught them both off guard. "All I know is, if we were out here alone…" He checked to make sure Riley was still in Top 40 land. Her rhythmic head bobs reassured him. "I'd give in to the temptation if we were here alone." Kissing her here in this peaceful cove… That might be heaven.

Might not. He'd never know until he tried.

Christina sat up slowly. "It's a good thing we have company, then." She turned away from him to put on her socks and shoes.

Pursuing the topic of conversation would not get him the response he wanted. That much was clear.

If he knew whether it was true disinterest or the fear of upsetting Leanne that stopped Christina, he might understand better how he felt. As it was, he was more confused now than when he'd gotten into the boat.

Time to call it a day.

"We're running out of good behavior time. And you're definitely going to be sunburned. Should head back." The sad pit in his stomach at the end of a beautiful day matched her face perfectly, but she didn't argue. Brett started the motor and made the quick trip back to the marina. Even Riley and Parker were quiet as they unloaded Ash's boat and piled back into the SUV.

"Come to dinner." The perfect day shouldn't end like this—sad and dissatisfying. Brett tightened his hands on the steering wheel, as uncertain around her as he had been as a kid. Then he'd wanted to save her, help her. Now he wanted to be with her.

"There he is again, Officer Hendrix, the man with the plan and orders to back it up," Christina said with the saucy grin that usually set his teeth on edge. "I'm amazed that such an upstanding member of the Smoky Valley Nature Reserve law enforcement team has been able to fight his real nature for so long, but you'll have to sweeten the deal to win me over. I was expecting a freshly caught fish fry tonight. You've let me down." She wagged her finger as a gust of wind from the open window tossed her ponytail across her face. Her spluttering turned into a rusty laugh and Brett was shocked at the fluttery, strange oddness in the center of his chest.

Christina Braswell was seductive and tough and sometimes hard.

At that moment, she was also adorable.

"No fish on the menu, but I'll do all the cooking, set the table and clean it up. No waiting or working for you." Christina deserved a nice dinner at a table with linen cloths and waiters in black ties. She deserved to be pampered. Every woman did. But he had to work with the hand he was dealt. She would find charred hot dogs and grape juice unique.

He certainly did.

"I'm not sure this is a good idea," Christina said as she motioned between them. It didn't take a lot of words to get the point across, but what he understood was that she felt the pull of attraction he did. If there were no Leanne, no tangled past between them, they'd plan a second date in the middle of the first one.

Because they clicked.

Without all that stress and anger and history, they worked. As long as he didn't study it too closely, he could see a hundred other sunny days on the lake with Christina. And morning coffee, helping with English homework while she did the science, attending school plays and football games, and eventually crashing on the couch together to reconnect after Riley and Parker were asleep.

All of that, he could see with Christina.

He was in deep, deep trouble. "Free food. No cooking. How can you pass that up?" He held his hands out as if to say "And nothing else, no pressure for things you don't want." That he was committed to. He could build the plan that suited him perfectly with Christina in the center, but he had a hard time listing what she'd get out of the bargain. So he would do his best not to push.

He owed her that.

And he owed caution to Leanne.

"A meal with no table bussing required afterward." She offered him her hand to shake. "Deal."

Her hand was strong and soft.

A lot like the Christina he'd seen that day on the lake.

"I'll grill. There will be meat. That's all I can promise." Brett pointed at her seat belt. "Buckle up. We wouldn't want to break the law."

She saluted and fastened the belt. He shot a look in the rearview mirror before he backed out of the parking spot. Riley and Parker each had earbuds in. His son was watching the video clip show on his phone. His obsession with the show might bother Brett, but he had an idea that Parker was studying it in order to win the prize someday. He hoped.

Riley's eyes were closed, but every now and then her lips moved as if she was fighting the urge to sing along.

For his kids, this was as good as good behavior got. All he had to do was make it through dinner without a meltdown and this would be the memory Christina had of a day with the Hendrix family. No drama. No anger.

This would be the kind of day they could build on.

Whether it was a friendship or more, he was happy to have something sweet to start with.

CHAPTER ELEVEN

IF SHE HAD been asked to describe the perfect day, it might have included an afternoon on Otter Lake and a dinner she didn't have to cook or clean up afterward. Christina wasn't sure it would have included Brett Hendrix, but anytime she had a chance to do so in the future, her plans might feature not only the man, but his kids prominently.

Even listening to them argue was charming.

Probably because she didn't have to do it day in and day out.

"Riley, set the table." Brett had rolled back the lid of an impressive gas grill and Christina could almost see the raw determination of the caveman settle over his shoulders. He was going to conquer fire and looked forward to every minute of it.

"Make Parker do it," Riley said from her

sprawled position in the swing. She held her phone in front of her face, and instead of rocking out with her playlist or even a friendly texting match, she was furiously texting, an angry snarl wrinkling her lips. "I'm busy right now."

"I'll be happy to—" Christina sat up abruptly when Brett directed his own snarl at Riley. This was what she didn't miss about family life. When they got along, everything was rainbows and unicorns. This tension made her restless in her seat.

"That can wait until after dinner," Brett said as he took her phone and pointed. "Set the table."

The ugly glares they exchanged before Riley stomped off made a hard knot in Christina's stomach. She'd been that girl.

Riley needed discipline. She had to listen to her father, the one man determined to keep her safe, but his tone… Christina bit her lip, half a second away from telling him how wrong he was.

"I know. That's not going to work with her." Brett turned toward her. "I know it and I do it anyway." He plopped the phone down on the table and turned back to his grill, all of the pleasure and determination gone from his posture.

"Oh, Riley is on the warpath now," Parker said in a loud, carrying voice as he stepped outside, arms weighed down with plates, cups and two pitchers of juice. "That buzzy bee better look out."

For the second time, Brett turned slowly away from the grill. "What did you say?"

Did Parker mean bee, like insects that pollinate, or another *B* word? In all the time she'd spent with the Hendrix kids, neither one of them had cursed in front of Christina. She'd always suspected that was because she was too far on the other side of the authority figure line.

Parker set his burden down with a satisfied nod. "Must be Naya she's talking about. If anyone is a queen bee, it's her. Always talking, buzz, buzz, buzzing and in charge of the girls on the bus." He wiped his nose on the back of his arm. "Did you know that some beekeepers mark the queens with paint? Yeah, different colors represent different years. We learned about it in a video at school." He shook his head sadly. "The bees are in trouble, guys."

As Parker talked, Christina could see Riley's phone lighting up with text after text. She reached over to pull it closer. Reading the girl's texts was definitely something she'd feel guilty about. Later.

Then she read the mean words coming in on a group text and she didn't regret a thing. She handed the phone to Brett and stood. "Where is Riley now?"

Parker motioned with his head. "Bathroom. She didn't ask where the clippers are this time, but from the buzzing inside, she remembered." He frowned. "Naya was the worst last week, Dad. You should have heard her ordering Riley to make her hair blue if she wanted to sit with them. Queen bees, girls who are supposed to be her friends, always talking about Riley and..." Parker glanced at his father and shook his head. Christina was certain her expression must match the confused frown on Brett's face. Then they were moving together. Both of them skidded to a stop next to the bathroom door.

Brett raised his hand to knock, but the audible sniffle froze his hand in place. Christina saw that Parker had followed them. If he'd been clueless before, he was picking up on the concern. A small frown wrinkled his forehead.

"Parker, could you go and set the table, please?" Christina asked.

"I did that already." Parker spun back and forth. "It was Riley's job."

"Then you could go and…" Christina made grasping motions.

"Go watch TV in your room. Dinner in ten minutes." Brett held up a hand because Parker was ready to argue.

Watching his son trudge down the hall, dejected because he was certain he was going to miss out on Riley's lecture, lightened the moment.

"Never waste time grasping for straws when a forceful order will do. You'd never make it as an officer," Brett muttered as he turned back to the door in front of him.

"He's very expressive," Christina whispered and squeezed Brett's shoulder. "He gets that from his mother's side."

They shared a grin, then Christina tapped on the door. "Riley, can I come in?"

Brett braced his arm on the door frame, relief on his face. He wanted to help, but he was out of his depth. Bullies were something she had experience with and that was going to come in handy.

If Riley would let her in.

The quiet snick of the door unlocking snapped Brett up straight.

Christina was just as surprised her gentle request had worked. Now she had to make the opportunity count.

After a stunned glance at him, Christina turned the knob and stepped inside.

Brett shifted left and right to catch a glimpse of Riley, but she was too clever and the door was closed again. If Christina had any money to bet, she'd throw it all on a gamble that Brett had his ear pressed to the door.

That would make Riley's shouting, "Go away, Dad," that much easier to hear.

He'd been desperate for help. She was here now. She'd give it everything she had. "Food, Brett. Everything is burning, you know. We're tired and hungry. We'll be out soon, but we all need food." She pressed her own ear to the door. After a minute, she heard him stomping back down the hallway.

Then she turned back to assess the damage.

As soon as she saw the blue locks on the floor, Christina understood why Riley was hiding in the bathroom. The blue streak that had first sent her into a nervous breakdown at the mere suggestion, and then had been finagled out of Brett at a low point, was lying on the bathroom floor, along with enough brown to give Christina heart palpitations.

"Oh, I'm interrupting a spa day." Christina eased down on the edge of the bathtub as she watched Riley sob from her spot on the toilet. She'd shaved a strip down the side of her hairline, which would have been cool if she was an '80s punk singer. At thirteen, it was a bit shocking.

It will all grow back. Christina repeated the mantra to herself. This was not the time to flip out over a bad haircut. There were bigger things at stake.

"Naya…" Riley gulped and shook her head as if she couldn't stand to see her own image. "She was supposed to be my best friend. I trusted her, but I don't want anything to do with her."

Christina eased down to the floor and crossed her legs. *Just be cool.*

"Her hair is blue and yours is…gone." Christina took a deep breath. "What happened?"

Riley ran her fingers over her stripe. "She…" The girl shook her head.

"Come on, tell me. I like to know what my enemies have done before I cross them off my list forever. Tell me what she did so I can be guilt-free about it."

"My *best friend* told everyone she could that Mom…" Riley licked her lips. "That she was a meth junkie." Fat tears rolled down her cheeks and she wiped her nose on her sleeve.

Christina immediately wished she'd let Brett handle this. It was a minefield she didn't want to maneuver.

But she'd wanted to watch over Riley and Parker. Surely, this was part of the price.

"She's not." Christina kept her voice low and calm. She was telling the truth as far as she knew. Leanne had been a sucker for pills, but meth was easy to come by. What if she'd decided to go for any high?

Would Christina know about it? Maybe, maybe not.

"I know!" Riley yelled. "But do you think anyone takes my side?"

Of course not. Once people had an idea of who they thought you were, they lost interest in the real you, especially if the real you was a regular person with the same hurts and fears as everyone else.

"I'm sorry for yelling." Riley blinked, misery plain on her face. "I can't believe I did something so stupid, but she was my best friend, Aunt Chris. It's still there." She tugged on the remaining blue strand.

Nobody could do heartbreak like a teenage girl. Christina sent up a brief prayer of thanks that she'd made it through herself.

And hugged Riley close, appreciating the rare "Aunt Chris" from her. Christina understood this pain. Waking up to find her car gone, taken by the woman she'd call a sister, had been a shock. Hearing her worst fears used as mean-girl gossip on the bus ride home would hurt so much more.

That made it easier to be patient with Riley, who was trying to make it to the other side of puberty in one piece.

Christina stepped up behind Riley and dug around in a drawer to find sharp scissors. The clippers were power tools meant for function, not style. Scissors were for precision. With a little care and attention, Riley's hacking could go from horror to hip.

"When your mom and I were going through this, when the people in town were determined to believe everything about us apart from what we knew to be true, we decided to change our style, too. Sweetwater was about cowboy boots and plaid—"

Riley snorted. "Still is."

She was absolutely right. "Still is. But we were going to look as different as we felt. Goth was the only way to go. Black hair. Black eyeliner. Black clothes. Black attitudes."

Riley's head snapped around, barely missing a seriously bad snip that would have changed her pixie into a mohawk on one side. Christina firmly turned her head back around. "Don't do that while I have scissors in my hand."

"I haven't ever seen pictures like that." Riley's narrowed eyes suggested she thought Christina was lying.

"That's because once I came out of the haze of rebellion, I made it my mission to find every single existing photo and destroy it. It's a real blessing social media wasn't around then." Christina relaxed a fraction as a wide grin transformed Riley's face. "Your mother? She looked like a Paris runway model in all that mess, while I would have gotten fired from a vampire movie for scaring the crew. It was so bad, Riley."

Riley paused as she processed that, and then giggles spilled out, bouncing off the tiled floor and walls until Christina was pretty sure the neighbors could hear them, but the relief was overwhelming.

She'd been there when Riley needed her. And she'd helped.

Her long weekend of parenting had seemed pretty thankless, but in this moment, Christina understood the reward. She was watching Riley mature right before her eyes.

Being a part of that was…

"So, I guess bad dye jobs happen." Riley nodded. "Thanks, Aunt Chris."

The nickname punched up the connection between them another notch.

"That was only part of the reason I told you that story." Christina pressed her hands on Riley's shoulders, grateful for the connection that she would do whatever it took to keep. "I'm also saying that your mother could rock any number of fashion mistakes and make the world think she'd chosen them on purpose. Thrift store dresses for picture day, the free T-shirts they hand out at car dealerships, the leather jacket she stole from a movie theater…she owned every bit of it. Whatever that is, you have it, too."

Christina waited for Riley to meet her stare in the mirror. "This haircut works for you. Whatever you choose next will, too, because you are a beautiful girl. Don't let anyone, not your ex–best friend or the town gossip or whoever else comes along, convince you you're any less."

Riley gulped and ran a hand through her spiky hair.

"You forget what they say, Riley, and know what you know. If you can learn that, you're going to save yourself a lot of heartbreak down the road," Christina said softly.

The older she got, the more Christina

understood that lesson herself, but she wanted the journey to be easier for Riley.

"Think she'll come home soon?" Riley asked.

That was the question, wasn't it?

"I hope so. Run, grab the broom before your father sees all this." Christina urged Riley to the door. As Riley charged toward the kitchen, a lanky streak in a hurry, Christina wondered if she had time to threaten Brett with death by violent means if he reacted poorly to his daughter's new hairstyle, but Riley's clomping steps signaled her quick return.

"He better have the burgers on. I'm starving," she said as she swept up the clouds of hair, all her tears seemingly forgotten. It was good to be young. The mountains faded back to molehills as quickly as they grew.

Nothing was solved, but Riley was ready to roll with the punches, get back up and move forward.

That attitude reminded her of Leanne, too.

"Let's go, Chris." Riley didn't look back as she left the bathroom.

In a hurry to win the race outside, Christina yelled, "Riley, grab the drinks." Then she darted down the hall and out to the deck, where she did her best to warn Brett with her eyes that he better not do or say anything to rock the boat she'd just gotten upright. He and Parker were staring down at the grill, deep in thought.

Or urging everything to cook faster.

Riley appeared, her shoulders hunched as if she was ready to protect herself. Christina clenched her hands together and willed Brett to be the nice guy who'd die for his daughter instead of the lawman determined to force everyone to fall in line.

Brett didn't disappoint.

He studied his daughter's hair and face carefully before turning back to flip the hot dogs. "New haircut. I like it. Makes you look so grown-up."

Like a flower stretching toward the sun, Riley straightened and moved closer to her father. "You think so?"

Without looking away from the grill, Brett wrapped an arm around Riley's shoulders and tugged her in for a hug. "I do."

Happy and relieved and sad Leanne was

missing this and appreciative that, no matter what, Brett loved his kids like the father she'd always wished she'd had, Christina closed her eyes and eased down in one of the cushy seats at their outdoor table. "Hey, Parks, is the grub almost ready?"

"You made it in time. Parker was about three seconds away from inhaling everything on the grill, and then coming after me. Don't stand between a boy and his food." Brett loaded up a plate with steaming hamburgers and hot dogs, Parker's favorite food above all else, and pointed at the table with his spatula. "Watch your fingers when he sits down."

"Hungry, hungry," Parker growled, and then held both hands out like he would grab the plate.

"I'd take his advice, Aunt Chris," Riley said as she slumped down in one of the cushy seats. "Kid eats enough to grow two more like him." The superior, slow shake of her big-sisterly, much-wiser head was so funny, but there was only one person on the deck to share the joke with.

As her eyes met Brett's, he blinked lazily and tipped his nose in the air, the perfect caricature of a worldly-wise teenager.

"Is that supposed to be me?" Riley drawled. Parker shot a glance up at his father before he shoved a hot dog loaded with ketchup into his mouth, and then sighed happily. "Because I do not look like that."

Brett frowned as if he couldn't imagine what she was talking about and Christina dipped her head to stare hard at her plate to keep from laughing. She was back in Riley's circle. It would not be a good idea to be caught teasing her.

"Go ahead. Don't choke yourself." Riley's lips were twitching as she took a delicate bite of her hamburger. "But be prepared to Heimlich the kid when he chokes on the second hot dog."

Brett reached over and scooted Parker's plate away. "Slow down, champ. Nobody's after the title tonight."

"Most hot dogs. Someday I'm gonna win a prize for eating the most hot dogs." Parker threw his hands in the air, jarring the table and sending his drink lurching to the side. Apparently this happened often enough that Brett was prepared. He caught the glass and set it upright without pausing in his own dinner.

Watching him with his kids like this... If she'd had any room in her hard heart for Brett Hendrix, this dinner with his kids would have filled it with warm emotion of some kind. He was calm, patient, and knew how to draw them out. He would never have been happy to leave them to someone else to raise.

How lucky Parker and Riley were to have him.

"Want to tell me what brought on the cut?" Brett asked casually, as if nothing was all that important. "You had me worried there for a minute."

Christina took a bite of the best hamburger she'd had in a long while—she wondered if she'd ever had one this good—and waited tensely. If anything would bring the wall between her and Brett slamming down again, it would be Leanne and her actions upsetting his kids.

Riley shrugged. "It's dumb. I needed a change."

Parker gulped down his juice, and then swallowed hard before he said breathlessly,

"Kids on the bus. They say Mom's doing something bad so she can take drugs." He waved the hot dog in his hand. "Don't know why it matters. It's not true." He chomped down the last bite of hot dog, satisfied that he'd scooped his sister and given his opinion correctly.

"What sort of bad things?" Christina asked.

Parker rolled his eyes. "Riley shoved the girls talking before I could figure that part out."

Riley met Christina's stare and she didn't have to say anything else. Anger flashed through Christina so quickly that she could feel her cheeks blaze. Leanne had given her enough trouble to last a lifetime, but the fact that kids would make up stories like that, stories that they'd no doubt picked up from the adults in their lives, it was wrong, plain and simple.

Christina set her hamburger down and clenched her hands together under the table.

"Anyway, no big deal," Riley said, "because for once in his life, Parker's right. They were lying, so who cares?"

Brett wiped his mouth with his napkin, a small frown wrinkling his brow. He cared. He'd always cared about what people said. He cared even more about the things that hurt his kids. He'd take this as confirmation that his decision to cut Leanne out of their lives was correct.

"Have either of you talked to Mom lately?" he asked breezily. Because she was watching, Christina saw Riley tense, but she shook her head.

"The worst part was Naya. She's supposed to be my friend. She should have my back." Riley chomped at her burger vigorously, showing her frustration.

Christina did some of her own angry chewing until all that was left of her hamburger was mutilated bun and a smear of mustard. Then she plopped back against her chair.

"I don't want to have anything like her." Riley tugged on the remaining blue hank of hair. "Guess I'll have to let this grow out."

"With the short cut, it shouldn't take too long." Brett crumpled up his napkin. "Then we can go back to the way things were." He sighed happily. "Just like Dad wants."

Riley snorted. "Or I'll go goth, like Aunt Chris and Mom did in high school."

Brett turned to Christina. "I'd forgotten all about that phase."

"Good. Forget about it again." Christina laughed as Brett bumped her shoulder. It was good to lighten the mood up, even at the expense of the reminder of her fashion mistakes.

"Well, I like the blue. It makes you look like a superhero," Parker said as he stood from his chair, both arms raised as if he'd take flight.

Riley's eyebrows rose. It must be surprising to hear an annoying little brother say something positive, but she rallied quickly enough. "No, you're the hero and I'm the villain, come to steal your...treehouse." Both kids shoved away from the table and hurtled down the steps to take up spots on the first-class treehouse Brett had built for Riley approximately three seconds after they'd moved into this house.

Parker was yelling his plans to defend his stronghold until death had claimed his last breath. Riley wasn't doing much more than darting forward and back now and then, but it was enough to keep them both entertained.

Brett stood and pressed both hands on the deck railing.

She remembered when he built it, too. In the early days of their move back to Sweetwater, when he'd still been trying to be the big brother she'd never had, she'd been cheap labor, carrying and toting in between entertaining Riley.

"Are they going to be okay?" Brett asked softly.

Christina paused in her clumsy efforts to pretend to be a good houseguest. She dropped the plates she'd stacked up back on the table and tipped her head up to stare at the dusky sky. Here, with nothing but the sound of happy kids and the creek that ran along the back of the property, they could pretend the rest of the world had disappeared.

"I don't know," she said as she stepped up to lean next to him, "but if any kids stand a chance, those two do."

Brett stared hard at her. He didn't say it but she could read the doubt on his face.

"Even with their mother's problems and

this town's...interest in those problems."
She grimaced. "We appear to have called a
momentary truce, so I'll go ahead and say
it. Riley and Parker are lucky to have you.
If anyone can raise two strong kids in this
messed-up world, you can do it."

He winced. "Not by myself."

"I'll help." Christina crossed her arms
over her chest. If he rejected her offer after
all they'd been through together, it would
break her. "I hope you can see that you can
rely on me."

He squeezed her shoulders. When he let
go, the fading warmth surprised a shiver
from her. Before she could figure out a way
to make him agree that she was the best
nanny to ever drive a rattletrap truck down
a mountain, he was gone. The door to the
kitchen was standing open, spilling warm
yellow light into the growing shadows of
the night.

"Or you can pretend I'm not speaking to
you and go inside," Christina muttered, and
then looked up as he trotted back through
the doorway.

"Here. Leanne hated these, but a better
clothing solution has not been invented."

He held out a flannel shirt. "Put this on. Now that the sun's going down, it'll get cooler."

Frustrated and amused at his undying chivalry, Christina slipped her arms inside. "I was doing my best to have a heart-to-heart with you, you know."

"I'm not good at those." He buttoned the top two buttons, and then rolled up the too-long sleeves.

"I'm not Parker's age." Unsettled by how close he was and how nice it felt to stand there in the shadow he cast, his warmth bleeding through the flannel into every place he touched her, Christina licked her lips. What was happening? "You can't help being a father, can you? It's in your blood."

Brett's lips were curled as he studied her face. "It is. I was meant to be a dad. I don't want to be your father or your brother or any of that anymore. You've proved to me you don't need a…knight or whatever. You fight your own battles."

His mouth was so close. Only one of Parker's shrieks could cut through their connection.

Christina stepped back and watched as

Parker and Riley swung upside down from a long bar that extended from the tree to the swing set. The urge to tell them to get down right now trembled on her lips, but she bit it back. Brett was the real parent; he was the expert in this situation. If he wasn't worried, she shouldn't be, either.

And they were half a second from coming to some kind of understanding. She wasn't certain about what, but there was something important here.

"You think I fight my own battles?"

"Absolutely." He nodded. "This last week you did some impressive coping when I needed you to."

She had. If they'd been two different people, she might have thought he admired her for that. It was a nice idea. If they hadn't spent decades tied together in a weird face-off over Leanne, what might they have been to each other?

"You said we'd talk about Leanne." It was now or never. The dark made it easier to ask. "Find out where she is for me. I'll go and get her. Whatever she's gotten herself into, we can fix it."

He was quiet so long that she was preparing her next argument. He was going to have to help her, though. Until he set the direction, she wasn't sure which reasoning made the most sense.

"How many times will you go after her, Chris?" He said the words quietly. That was a good thing because his kids had decided they'd been unplugged entirely too long and came rushing up onto the deck.

Before they could disappear inside, he said, "Pick up the dishes and put them in the dishwasher, please. Then you can watch television." They grumbled as they went and had nearly made it over the threshold to safety when he added, "After you do your homework."

Parker whined until Riley said, "Come on. I'll help you."

Christina was surprised until Brett added, "Really help him this time, you con man."

The girl's long-suffering sigh reminded Christina of the same from Leanne a million times over.

Christina was smiling as she moved to sit in her favorite spot, the porch swing with the creaky chains. Then Brett settled next to her. It was the right size for the two of them in the quiet night. As he set the swing in motion, it was tempting to pull her feet under her and lean her head on his shoulder.

"Riley and I used to swing here every night. Before she got so mature." His disgruntled tone was sweet and funny. If she spent too much more time with the Hendrixes, she'd find all of Brett's hidden, attractive facets.

This was dangerous, but she was too relaxed to run.

"You asked how many times I'd go after Leanne." Christina took a deep breath, and then let it go. She wasn't going to fight this. "Every time. There's not one time I wouldn't go after her, because she's family. The only family I have. I'm not going to drop that. Ever."

He didn't answer. It was interesting to sit next to Brett, to know that he was turning her words over in his mind, really considering them, and to not have a single worry about the outcome. In this, she had no regrets.

"For a woman who left you behind. That's how you feel about her still?" Brett draped an arm over the back of the swing, the weight a warm blanket across her shoulders.

"Always. Even if we were separated by years and miles, I'd go when she needed me. Just like you will for Riley and Parker." Just like he might for Leanne if Christina could convince him that this was a woman who needed a knight. "You don't have to do anything but use whatever resources you have to track her down. I'll go. I'll convince her to come home."

"I don't expect you to get this, but there's part of me that wonders if we aren't better off if she stays…gone. Including you, too. For years, you've been stepping in for her. What would happen if you only had to do for yourself?"

It was a question that she'd considered often, especially after her best friend had stranded her without a car.

"Doesn't matter. I'm who I am because she's part of my life. I'm not going to forget that. If I'd been in the same situation as a kid that Riley was in today, there's no way Leanne would have turned on me. Naya's a kid and she saw a means to get out of the spotlight, so she flipped. Leanne in the same position, she'd have come out swinging for me. This is how I'm doing the same for her." It was so simple. How could he have any trouble understanding it?

"How lucky she is to have you in her corner." Brett eased the swing into motion again, each easy forward rock shifting them closer together.

"Help me. If you value the things I've done, help me find her." Christina wasn't sure what she'd do once she had the missing info, but it didn't matter. "It's been too long. All I can imagine is her confused and helpless against the addiction with no one to help." While she was living the cozy, happy life of a Hendrix, Leanne was all alone.

"I said I'd help and I will, but…"

"This isn't enabling." Christina was too tired to shout, but she hoped he understood her. "I wasn't enabling her those nights at the Branch, either. We talked. We laughed. We stared down handsy tourists and we ate junk food. That's it. Saving and supporting, and feeding, if she's hungry, and even giving up a car…" Christina cleared her throat. "I don't have to love it. I have to *do* it. Because I love her."

"That fight about the Branch. That was the last straw, huh?" Brett sighed.

"You told her not to call or see her kids. If anything can be a last straw..." That would be it.

Now that she'd spent time with him, she'd gotten to know him better, but if anything happened to Leanne because of that straw, they would never recover.

"I'll get an address. With Ash's help, we should be able to track her down."

She studied his face. "I'll go. I'll find her. If it's bad, I'll...take care of it. I don't want Parker and Riley hurt, either."

Brett nodded. "But what about you, Chris?"

The question caught her off guard and tears sprang to her eyes before she knew they were coming. "I'll be fine. No matter what, I can handle it."

It was true. She might wonder how she'd ever dig out of the financial hole she perpetually fell back into, no matter how hard she worked, but she had no doubt that she could handle whatever life threw at her.

But to do it, she needed Leanne.

And Brett. Riley and Parker made the struggle worthwhile. This connection was what she'd been missing.

"I wish you weren't so certain that nothing could knock you down." Brett wrapped a hand around her shoulder and squeezed. "Certainty like that comes from too much struggle."

Christina laughed. "It also means you can't tell me anything, not anymore, Sir Knight. And you hate that."

His disgruntled note was a sweet sound in the shadows of the early evening. Brett ran a hand over his jaw, the sound of his past–five o'clock shadow whispered through the night. "I could never fall for a woman who won't let me charge to her rescue, you know."

Startled, Christina jerked, rattling the chains holding the swing. "Who said anything about falling?"

"Definitely not you." Brett pulled his arm off the back of the swing and leaned forward to brace his hands on his knees. "All day, I couldn't ignore the fact that you and I have this easiness between us—that's what I want. Forever. Not for an afternoon. You love my kids. You keep me on my toes without making me suffer for every slight. And you're strong enough that nothing and no one would budge you from where you wanted to be."

"But…" This pull she'd been experiencing… It had to be about a comfortable house and a sweet family. If he was feeling it, too, then there was more at stake. She stared at him on the swing. He had stubble, messy hair, lake clothes and a grim expression. And all she wanted to do was wrap his arm around her shoulders so she could snuggle into his side and stare up at the stars.

He slowly bent his head toward hers but froze at the last second. "I promised myself I wouldn't do this. Friends. I need them. You do, too, but…" His breath mingled with hers and it was impossible to turn away from him. Christina pressed her mouth to his, raising her temperature and the need to get closer to him. She wrapped her hands in soft flannel and sighed as his arms settled her against his chest. A prince could ride up on a white horse with a fistful of jewels in one hand and the keys to a castle in the other, and she'd feel nothing.

The chance to kiss like this, to talk and swing and tackle all the coming struggles together with this infuriating, admirable man—that was temptation.

"Hey, Dad, can I…" Riley's shout died as she stumbled to a stop on the deck. She immediately tried to smooth a loose strand of hair behind one ear and focused on the ceiling.

"What do you need, Riley?" Brett asked as he leaned away from Christina.

Riley tipped her chin up. "Never mind. It's not important." She disappeared inside before Christina could figure out what to say.

"Yeah. That's part of the 'but' you were going for, I guess." Brett stood to pace into the golden yellow rectangles of light spilling out on the deck. "I can't make decisions just for me."

He stopped and faced her. "But I want to. For the first time in so long, I know what I want. Together, we could work this out." He waited for her to answer and finally added, "Couldn't we?"

Suddenly too tired and sad to continue the conversation, Christina stood. "We don't have to make a decision this second." Slamming the door on the possibility, one that would give her everything she'd been dreaming of her whole life, or at least, ever since she'd understood that other families might be dysfunctional, too, but they were happy. So she tried to leave the door open, only a tiny crack. "First, I need to get Leanne home." And talk to her about all that had happened in nearly a month, and then find out...

The fact that she hoped that Leanne might ever be okay with her and Brett in a relationship convinced her how badly she wanted it.

That was a dangerous spot to be in. Wanting something that badly inevitably led to heartbreak.

"I'll do what I can. I'll also talk to Riley." Brett held a hand out as if he'd touch her again and Christina shook her head. It was a late night after a beautiful day. The easiest thing to do would be to give in to her feelings, but she'd learned a long time ago not to be weak like that. Her safety had depended on it; now her sanity did.

"I want to tell her good-night." Christina eased past him, half-tempted to hesitate so he could convince her to stay. *Strong. Be strong.* That was the only constant that had seen her through. She could always rely on herself.

Brett didn't follow as Christina walked slowly down the hall. Riley's room was quiet. There was no music, no giggling. Christina hesitated. Maybe Riley was already asleep. The line of light seeping under the door made it impossible to turn away in good conscience, so she tapped lightly.

"It's me. Christina. I'm leaving, but I wanted to tell you goodbye first." She tipped her head closer to the door, ready to answer the faintest invitation.

Instead, the door swung open. "Trying on the role of mommy, are you?" Riley propped her shoulder against the doorjamb, arms crossed firmly over her chest. "I was beginning to think you were my friend. I should have expected you had an ulterior motive."

This had been what she was afraid of. That Riley had gotten the wrong idea, but Christina hadn't expected such an aggressive confrontation.

"I *am* a friend. I will never be a mommy, your mommy, no matter what happens. Aunt Chris." Christina patted her chest. "That's who I am. Nothing about that has changed."

"Except for the kissing. And don't even try to convince me that was anything else." Riley snorted. "I'm young, not dumb."

"I hope you can still depend on me to tell you the truth." Christina ran her hand through her hair and realized her ponytail was listing hard to the side. She gave it a yank. "And I have to figure out what that is for myself first, before I can answer anything for you. Neither one of us planned it, okay?"

"But you aren't saying it won't happen again." Riley's suspicious glare now had a touch of her father.

"I can't." Christina laughed. "And the fact that I'm even saying that…" She clasped both hands to her head. The whole day had been a wild ride of things that she'd never expected. Why would the last hours be any different?

"What about my mother?" Riley asked, worry clear in her eyes. "You're what she's got now, Chris."

"Always. I will be her friend always, Riley. As soon as I find out where she is, I'll go and bring her home. I promise." As much as she'd wanted Brett's kiss, she wanted Riley to have faith in her. The kid needed to know that she had people in her corner. Riley should be shocked when adults let her down instead of prepared. "Hug me like you mean it and I'll go home. Otherwise, I'll stand here in your doorway. Your dad will get mad, yell about how I'm corrupting innocents again, and what a drag that will be. Parker will lose some of his beauty sleep, which would—" Riley's hard squeeze around Christina's middle halted the flow of words, which was a good thing. Coming up with more nonsense after the day she'd had would be too much.

"As soon as I know anything about your mother, I'll let you know." The promise bothered her a bit. Good news would be delivered quickly. Anything else would not.

Riley nodded and stepped back. "If it makes you feel better, I like you so much more than a teacher. Dad was planning to introduce us to his girlfriend and she was a teacher. He told us that like it was a good thing. I spend enough of my day with teachers, you know? Who wants to face one over a dinner table?" Riley shrugged as she closed her bedroom door and it was hard to argue with her logic.

It would be the same as waiting tables at the campground and coming home to dinner with Woody. Way too much of a good thing.

Brett had been hoping to have a teacher as their stepmother. What a drop down Christina must be.

Unless they both came to their senses and he returned to his original plan.

Brett was waiting by the front door. He wordlessly opened it for her and followed her after she stepped outside. The stars were so close on a clear night. It was like Mother Nature wanted to be certain that romance had a shot on White Oak Lane that evening.

Do not stop. Walk to the truck. Get

in. Go home. Get your head screwed on straight and some rest. Then hold him to his promise.

That was the only way through this tangle.

Once Leanne was home, then Christina could make clearheaded decisions.

Brett waited silently at the end of the driveway until she opened the door and slid inside. "Sleep well." Those were his only words. He could have been a hotel clerk checking her in for a one-night stay for all the feeling they carried.

Relief settled over her and she could see the amusement on his face.

He'd known exactly what she needed: an easy goodbye.

As knights went, he was proving more perceptive than she expected. He wanted to fight, but he could also hand her a shield.

Frustrated with herself and him, the feelings that she didn't want and never wanted to live without, Leanne, always Leanne, and so many things, Christina raised her hand, and then winced at the loud groan the truck made as she hit the gas.

Nothing about this situation included

shining armor, but she'd never doubt his heart.

He'd kissed her. She'd like to give him the benefit of the doubt and blame the romantic setting, but she and Brett were not made for romance.

He'd kissed her. He understood all the problems they were facing and he'd kissed her anyway.

Because he had to do it.

How often did people luck into that kind of attraction? And with a man who was so strong, a good guy who worked hard at a job he was great at and only wanted to love his family with the rest of his days?

That had never happened to her.

Christina was sure it would never happen again.

What kind of fool would run away from that?

As she left Brett's street and made the turn toward her cabin, Christina knew it was going to be a long night. Her whole world had shifted. She had to get it back on track by morning.

CHAPTER TWELVE

LEARNING HOW MUCH she appreciated routine had taken some adjustment, but it was never clearer to Christina as she drove up to the campground diner that morning. There was value in knowing her spot in the world.

Woody was sitting on the bench beside the door. He would order pancakes and burned bacon.

She could see Luisa's compact car and the junker Monroe drove parked around the side.

Sunshine was peeking over the mountaintops.

Misty clouds hung above the surface of Otter Lake.

And she was five minutes late.

All in all, it was as easy as easy could be to catch her breath. Brett and his kiss and the conflicting emotions spending time with the Hendrixes gave her belonged to some other woman's life. Here there was no need to explore her feelings or to worry that she was doing too much for Leanne or not enough.

Here she could slide into the routine and know that the world kept turning.

"Good morning, Woody." As his eyebrows rose, Christina realized she'd almost hit chipper and neither one of them had expected it.

"Well, now… I expect a day out on the lake has shaken some of them gloomy ol' cobwebs loose. I know it does for me." Woody's grin was contagious, so she answered with one of her own. "Things is lookin' up?"

That question was impossible to answer, so Christina opened the door. "Let's get you some coffee and bacon, friend." She waved at Luisa and Monroe and tied on her apron. As she poured Woody's coffee, her phone rang.

Since the morning rush was off to a slow start, she pulled her phone out to check who was calling. From now on, her first thought would always be that Brett had some kind of emergency. She wanted to be his first call every time.

When she saw Leanne's number, Christina stopped in her tracks.

Without warning Woody or Luisa, Christina turned on her heels and headed for the shady deck running down the side of the diner. Guilt and worry tangled together in a hard knot in her stomach. As soon as she stepped outside, she answered, "Hello? Did you think I'd lost my phone?" Christina asked, and forced a smile into her voice. "The week's been crazy. Sorry I didn't call you sooner."

She'd hoped going on the offense would throw Leanne off her game.

"I was afraid you'd finally decided the people in town were right," Leanne answered, a weird tremor in her voice. "It's only a matter of time."

"Oh, Lee. That isn't true." Christina rubbed the ache pounding in the center of her forehead while she tried to find the right words.

"He should have called me. Brett should have called me. I would have come home and taken care of Parker. You know I would." Leanne sniffed again. Christina couldn't tell if they were tears or something else.

"Come home now." Christina softened her words. There would be time someday to fight over who should have done what. Leanne was wrong. When she was herself, she'd see that, but not now. "I want you here. Your kids want you here. The only way Brett will ever do what you want is if you stay here and show him how much you care for those kids."

"Why should I have to?" Leanne yelled. "They're my kids. Of course I care for them. I love them. How can you say that to me?"

Slow and easy. That was the only way to talk to her. Christina had learned that during the bad times before. Under the influence, Leanne was determined to be angry and hurt.

"It isn't about loving them. You know that." Christina held her breath. "It's about being dependable. That's all. He has no one, Lee, not a single adult who he can call. If you could be that for him…" How much would everyone's life change?

"He has you, though." The tremor was back in Leanne's voice.

"Because he's desperate. I'm here." Christina pressed her hand to her forehead, confused over how best to continue the conversation. "And I'm sober." She was desperate to hear an angry, fiery retort in self-defense. The tense silence on the other end provided no relief.

"What should I have done?" Christina asked. "Refused to help?"

"Of course not," Leanne snapped, "but after all the things I did for you, you can't answer my calls or help me see them? My kids need me. Brett will poison them against me. He already has. Riley only answers one out of every four or five calls I make."

"And Parker?" Christina asked, the dread immediate. When Brett found out Leanne was calling the kids, he would not be happy.

"I haven't called. He's been sick." The lightning-fast changes in Leanne's tone used to confuse and distract Christina.

Now she understood that this tone in particular, the righteous one, was a sure-fire way the addict she loved like a sister manipulated her.

"Because he would never be able to keep the calls a secret from his father." Christina took a deep breath, determined to end the confession before she lost her footing. Leanne did her best to argue, but Christina talked over her. "Come home. I'll help Brett and Parker and Riley in the meantime, but don't ask me for anything else until you come back to Sweetwater."

She was half a second from ending the call, but she heard Leanne say, "I never thought you'd join them, all those people who hate me. That you'd do this to me while I'm here, fighting to…" She cleared her throat. "Were you waiting for me to leave to move in with Brett? Have you two had a thing going on? How long? How long have my husband and best friend been laughing at me behind my back?"

Her friend's shrill tone sent cold chills down Christina's back. That quick change? Christina could remember that unpredictability. Dread settled over her and Christina realized she was breathing in shallow pants. She gripped the wood railing, in desperate need of an anchor. "Lee, come on. You know better than that."

"What I know is that I'm hearing all kinds of stories now. A week ago, I couldn't get anyone to answer my calls. Now I can't stop them from calling me. Engaged? I didn't believe it at first, but Riley seems to think there's something going on between you. She begged me to call her, told me she needed advice on what to do about you two. I'm here, doing my best to… Well, trying to follow the rules and everything. What are you doing to my family, Chris?"

Christina's legs turned weak and she slid to sit on the deck. "You've got to listen, Leanne. Nothing is going on between me and Brett. I've been helping him with the kids. I had a dumb misunderstanding in the grocery store that led to the crazy engagement story, but no one with three functioning brain cells would buy it. I stayed with Riley and Parker while Brett was in Nashville. You knew that. As a…thank-you, he invited me to join them on the lake, and then he grilled. Burned hamburgers and hot dogs, that's all that's between us." Everything else between them? She didn't know what to call it.

"That's all." Leanne's voice was so quiet that Christina could hear what sounded like the overhead announcements that made it impossible to get any rest in the hospital. "What about the kiss?"

Christina squeezed her eyes shut. Riley had to have told her mother about that.

"Did Riley call you, Leanne?" She wasn't sure how strongly Brett would enforce his no-contact rule, but it wouldn't make him happy, not while they had no idea where Leanne was.

"Texted. She texted me in a panic, certain I was being betrayed just like Naya had let her down." Leanne sighed. "I have no idea what's going on with my kids, or my best friend, the only family I have. Do you know how that feels, Chris?" Her voice was calmer, but shaky.

Christina didn't know exactly, but if she were in the same place, there was no doubt it would tear her apart. If the previous night had been the last time she ever got to see Parker and Riley again, Christina would spend the rest of her life missing them, wondering who they had become. "Come home, Leanne. Nothing has changed. Brett and I are tolerating each other now, and your kids are awesome, but this is still home. You'll see. Tell me where you are and I'll come get you. Do you need money? Are you sick?"

Leanne was quiet so long that Christina was afraid she was done with the call.

"I can't come home, not yet. One week." Leanne laughed. "Home. Do I even have one anymore?"

"Sure you do. You'll crash with me at the cabin, like old times. Then, together, we'll go back to Brett. Whatever dumb rules he wants to put in place for your visits and how you'll act on the straight and narrow, we'll agree to. I'll help you meet them and you'll be taking Riley and Parker out for burgers in my car in no time." Christina held her breath. This tactic had worked in the past, the promise that everything would return to normal. It wasn't that Leanne couldn't see that Christina was doing her best to handle the situation. She had to believe it. And Christina had to have enough faith for the both of them.

Right now, she was struggling.

"You kissed him, Chris." Leanne sucked in a harsh breath. "I can't understand that. He's the reason I'm away from my kids. Don't you remember how arrogant he is, ready to think the worst? How many times did you tell me how much better off I'd be after the divorce?"

"Well, the guy who's drowning under raising two kids all alone is different from the Brett you might remember," Christina snapped. The urge to defend Brett was shocking. Her whole life, Leanne had been the only other person on her team. Over the past week, Christina had nailed the audition to be a part of the Hendrix team. "And you're both better off now, even...where we are. Tell me I'm wrong. Tell me you aren't better now than locked in an angry stand-off with him over the breakfast table." She knew it was true. They never should have gotten married, except Riley and Parker made all this turmoil worthwhile.

"I guess you think you could do better than I did." Leanne's bitter laugh was cut off. "I have to go."

"I love you more than chocolate milk

shakes, Leanne. Don't you ever doubt that."
Christina held the phone tightly and willed
Leanne to answer. The game she played
with Parker had started when she and Leanne were kids. Then they'd filled in the
blank with things they never thought they
might have: pearls, sports cars and Holly-
wood mansions.

They'd come so far together.

"I love you more than…freedom." Leanne's voice caught on the word, sending another alarm through Christina. "I'll
see you soon." The phone clicked with the
ended call before Christina was ready.

She stared at it so long that she failed
to notice the blur of tears that spilled over
and ran down her cheeks. Numb to the cell
phone clutched in her hand.

What was she going to do?

Only Luisa opening the door to the deck
snapped her out of the daze.

"You okay, *chica*? So pale." Luisa propped
her hip on the door frame. "Want I should
call Denise in? We ain't got a typical Monday crush, but it's more than I can handle
on my own."

Christina shook her head and brushed

the tears off her cheeks. "Yeah. I'm coming. I need the work."

Luisa's sympathy was difficult to face, but when she wrapped an arm around Christina's shoulders and squeezed hard, it was enough to land Christina right back in the real world.

"Work, it gets us through some dark times, I will say that," Luisa murmured, "but you need the time, you take it. You give enough that we can stand to do some giving ourselves, you know? I'll hand Monroe the coffeepot, have him giving directions to the tourists." Since it was hard to imagine the kid stringing a full sentence together, Christina smiled up at Luisa.

"That seems drastic." Christina ran her hands over her ponytail and stared out over the lake. The quiver in her fingers would make taking orders a challenge.

"Survivors, they get bad news, they stand back up and they go to work." Luisa offered her a hand to shake. "I knew you were one the minute you stepped inside the place."

Christina shook her hand and wondered if being called strong was going to get as old as all the usual compliments about how pretty she was. Didn't matter. It hadn't gotten stale yet.

Christina took her order pad out of her pocket. "Let's do this."

Luisa chuckled and followed her into the diner.

Putting Leanne's call out of her mind took real effort, but it was nice to have a steady stream of customers to help with that.

That warm glow of appreciation faded a bit as a rowdy group of fishermen took up the corner booth, and then Janet Abernathy and her friend Regina Blackburn sashayed in. She'd accepted that the locals were here to see what surprises she might pull off, whether there might be a Brett and Christina scene, but the woman who'd started the rumor partially responsible for Leanne's phone call was not high on her list of favorite people.

And what about the woman who enjoyed that kiss so much she'd do it again?

"What can I get you," she asked as the fishermen studied the menus.

"One second, sweetheart," the guy clearly

in charge of the others said with a smarmy smile, "although some hot coffee is always a fine way to start." He tapped the menu. "And you can put this all on my ticket."

Oh, my, you great big spender. The voice inside her head was rebounding from Leanne's call more quickly than the rest of her. Already so tired it was hard to stand, Christina turned toward Janet Abernathy's table. "It's good to see you again, Ms. Abernathy." Christina dug around in the pocket holding her skimpy tip money and pulled out five wadded dollar bills. "I can repay my debt and bring you a hot breakfast, one efficient morning's work."

"I wish you'd keep that, pay it forward for someone else who needs it, but I am not going to waste any more words, you hear? I spend enough time arguing with hardheaded people to recognize a lost cause." Janet waved her hand, and then held up the menu. "What do you think, Regina? What are we having?"

"We've been in here weekly for so long that we could recite the menu." Regina rolled her eyes and tucked one smooth strand of hair behind her ear. "Biscuits and gravy, heavy on the gravy." She wrinkled her nose. "At this age, we don't worry so much about clogged arteries."

Christina smiled as she slid the money across the table to Janet. "Coming right up."

Before she could escape, Janet held up one perfectly manicured finger. Hot pink flashed and caught Christina's attention, so she stopped. "We'd also like to discuss a business opportunity with you."

The loud clearing of a throat, universal signal of impatient diners everywhere, distracted Christina for a second. As she turned back to the fishermen, the important one with all the money to throw around waved and pointed at his table. "We're ready to order."

As common as the attitude was, Christina had to force a polite expression. "Certainly. I'll be right there."

The look on Janet Abernathy's face might have provoked a solid laugh, but she had no time. "Business opportunity?"

"Well, you know we're opening a spot downtown." She waved her hands, hot-pink nails flashing. "Mainly a real convenient place for tourists to pick up their magnets and their bumper stickers and their shot glasses... Travel souvenirs and what have you. In the same spot, we're planning a little sandwich shop and—"

The fisherman was now waving his menu in the air. "Burning daylight, hon."

Before Christina could answer, Janet stood up slowly. "Around here, parents teach their children to wait. Their. Turn. Hon." She smiled sweetly. "She'll be right with you, you hear?"

Instead of arguing, Janet's opponent settled back in his seat. The eyebrows of his companions were raised to the bills of their lucky fishing hats.

"We need a manager. Won't be a lot of food, but we need some help running the place." Regina shot a nervous look at Janet, who had not released the table of fishermen from her steely stare.

"And you want me to..." Christina couldn't even imagine what was taking place.

"Manage it. Run it. Help us, anyway." Regina waved her hands. "We have too many other irons in the fire to be there daily."

Christina fiddled with her order pad. Management? She'd never dreamed of anything like that. "How flexible is the schedule?" She wanted to make sure that whatever happened, she could help with Riley and Parker. And losing her daily shot of Otter Lake's peace would hurt.

"Well, you'll be the main staff, so..." Regina wrinkled her nose. "We'd work it out."

Overwhelmed by what should have been such an easy, normal day taking such strange twists, Christina said, "Why me?"

Janet shook her head. "You have impressed me. We need someone impressive in that spot."

"You should see the people applying for this job." Regina leaned forward. "Some of them have business degrees and everything." She said it like it was a dirty word. "We want somebody who knows Sweetwater and these mountains. Simple."

As she studied the women's faces, she could come up with a list of reasons why they should go with someone else. At the top of the list was her inexperience, and following right behind that was the love-hate relationship she had with the town.

"I know you've had a hard go, but you've got the spirit we want," Janet said, her eyes locked on Christina. "Now if you don't get those boys their coffee, they're liable to have an embarrassing hissy fit right here in the diner in front of God and everybody." She tsked her disapproval. "We can wait a few days for your answer, but I'm desperate for some gravy."

The tingling in her fingers was an indication that numbness was heading her way again, so Christina paused, regrouped, and then switched her brain off. Waiting tables was about constant movement and taking good notes. She could do both. By the time she'd served all her tables, refilled coffee and traded a bit of banter with Woody, some of the normal was returning and it was easier to believe she was going to survive that day.

Then she saw the reserve SUV arrive in the parking lot. Given how her luck was running, it couldn't be any other park employee. When her eyes locked with Brett's through the glass, Christina realized she was no closer to any decision than when she'd shown up that morning, but the time to act had come.

She had about fifteen seconds to make some life-changing decisions.

CHAPTER THIRTEEN

BRETT NEARLY STUMBLED to a stop as he watched Christina wipe a fingertip quickly below each eye. Was she crying? He could handle a lot of things. Guys who thought it was exciting to argue with a park ranger were a pain in the neck and more common than they should be. He'd dealt with two different sets that afternoon.

But Christina was supposed to be tough, strong. What would change that?

There was only one person in the world who could bring out tears. Christina had talked to Leanne.

"I would say good morning, but I can already tell that would be a lie." Christina had charged out the double doors of the restaurant and stood on the sidewalk. She seemed pale, brittle. Her expression? He'd call it "ready to fight" and he honestly could not understand how they were already back to square one. They were beyond that surely, or they should be. "I'm guessing you talked to my ex."

He wrapped his hand around Christina's elbow and guided her over to the bench. The way she folded, as if every bit of starch was gone and she was nothing but a shadow, worried him. "Tell me."

He propped his elbows on his knees, determined to be patient. Ash was expecting him again, since it was his first day back at work, but there were times when a man had to slow down. Whatever had happened, he needed to know.

"Someone called her and told her we were together. She knows about the kiss and…" Christina's voice broke, but she cleared her throat. "This might be it, Brett. If she relapses, how will we get her back? There's no home to keep her safe. Ever since the last time, I've worried that…" She covered her face with one hand.

"You don't have to say it. I know those worries." He squeezed her shoulder. "I shouldn't have put this off. This is me, being my old, unbending self. I will get an address today if there's any way to do it. Then we'll go. On one condition." He waited for her to look at him. "We'll do this one last time, Chris. We'll track her down and get her clean and set her up, but then we've got to…" Brett rubbed his forehead. "We have to live our lives. We'll do this and that's all we can do."

Christina didn't agree or disagree, but the wrinkle between her eyebrows suggested she was processing.

"Don't torment yourself over what might be happening. By this time tomorrow, we'll know." He hoped he could take his own advice, but if Leanne was in danger because of his stiff-necked pride and certainty that he knew how the whole world should live, Christina would never forgive him.

"That kiss. It was a mistake." She barely faced him. "It won't happen again. We aren't right together."

Brett tilted his head back. Such a beautiful, sunny day to lose everything he'd only recently realized he wanted.

She stood slowly. "I can't believe you'd give up on her. Ever."

"For as long as we've known each other, we've been locked in a battle of wills. If mine is strong, yours is stronger. You've managed to take care of yourself when you had no help and yet you've helped Leanne, too. The thing is, I'm not sure we've battled over something I want as badly as I want a chance to see what we might have between us."

She snorted, not because she was amused. "Right. What we might have between us could be about six exciting months, and then decades of fallout. Sound familiar?"

"You aren't Leanne. You've listened to too much Sweetwater gossip if you think that." Brett wasn't sure of the right direction to go, but it was impossible to read her mind when she kept her face turned away. "You've managed what you have through grit and determination, not trickery or manipulation. You're different, Christina."

She closed her eyes. "And that's where you lost me. The only opinion that counts is yours, right? The man has decided that I am worthy of his attention and thus will convince others around him to follow that reasoning. Well, we have the same background, Leanne and I. We have the same hurts. We made so many of the same mistakes. She was the one who was smart enough to focus on you, Brett. Even at seventeen, I knew we'd all end up here." She bit her lip. "Maybe you're right about part of this. We get her through this, and then there is no more 'we.'" She studied the lake over his shoulder. "I'm going to miss that view, but it may be time to leave Sweetwater in the rearview mirror." She shook her head. "If I ever get my car back."

Brett tried to take her hand, but her cold stare stopped him. "I don't know what she said, but there's no need to pack up and leave. This will blow over."

"And in this happy ending you've invented, we go on our merry way while Leanne is magically all better."

"The point is we don't spend the rest of our lives picking up her pieces. I've spent enough time doing that." He held out his hands. "I want to be happy, Chris. We could be."

"Not if that 'we' excludes her. Your kids, Brett. Leanne will always be your family. Do you get that? And *she's* desperate for a knight." Christina wrapped her arms tightly over her chest. "Why won't you offer her the service you try and try and try to push on me?"

Whatever argument he might have made, she cut off. Christina lurched up from the bench. "I don't have time for more conversation. Find out where she is. Keep your promise to me. I'll go get her, return your truck, and then... Well, we'll have to see where we all go from there."

Brett stood. "Fine. For now, I agree."

"For now." Her lips were a tight line. "Until you can convince me to go along with you. Where have I heard something like that before?" She tapped her chin. "Oh, yeah, it was my knight in shining armor. He was pretty sure he could love me if only I'd change everything about myself." She yanked the diner door hard. "But who needs a knight?"

Brett watched her disappear inside, completely dumfounded at how the morning had derailed so quickly.

Confused over what to do next, he paced along the sidewalk until Janet Abernathy and Regina Blackburn walked out of the restaurant. He did his best to appear pleasant as he nodded at them. "Ladies."

"Now, that is the face of one befuddled gentleman," Regina said as she stopped in front of the large Cadillac that was usually taking up two spots along the main street in town. "A bear who can't reach his honey."

The last thing he wanted to do was trade banter with two women who were solid representatives for the source of some of his trouble. Leanne had hated the way people in Sweetwater looked at her. His angry orders might have sent her over the edge, but she'd been clinging to the ledge for too long.

"Heard any good gossip lately?" Brett asked as he propped his hands on his hips.

Their slow blinks would have been funny if his whole world hadn't imploded.

"No, sir, but I am always a sympathetic ear." Janet's polite smile didn't hide the mad building behind her expression.

"Have a good day, ladies," Brett snapped as he stomped around them. Confronting Janet about the story she'd circulated would accomplish nothing at this stage.

Christina was in the corner with a group of tourists who'd had to have a stern lecture about steep drops and the dangers of the selfie stick the afternoon before. Glaring in their direction felt doubly good.

"Two pieces of pie, two coffees to go," Luisa said from her spot behind the cash register. "Your usual, Officer?" She raised one eyebrow and Brett wondered for a split second if Christina had told the diner's manager how to irritate him, if she'd picked it up from their previous exchanges, or, like Christina, she had a natural talent for tweaking authority without pushing too far.

He pulled out a ten and dropped it in her hand before he yanked the bag off the counter and carefully balanced the two coffees. Making a dramatic exit was impossible, thanks to the possibility of scalding burns and a wet uniform, so he slowly, deliberately stepped out on the sidewalk and definitely did not look back to check to see if Christina was watching.

If he had to glance in the window as he backed out of the parking spot, it was just good driving habits.

And she wasn't watching him anyway. Leaving black skid marks and the smell of burned rubber in the parking lot was tempting. Then he remembered he was in the reserve's SUV and he wasn't seventeen anymore.

Brett forced himself to ease up on the gas as he headed up to the ranger station. Another report of speeding through the reserve would not make his boss happy, and that would mean both of them would be mad as hungry bears in January.

"Good morning. How are you? I'm fine. How are you? Great. Thank you for asking. Would you like to come to dinner tonight? I have more hot dogs to burn. I'd like that. I could bring my pretty smile with me. Please do. I will. See you later. Can't wait." Brett gripped the steering wheel until it squeaked. "How hard is it to have a pleasant conversation? People do it all over the world. Strangers meet on the street and exchange more in conversation than we do."

Two mindful deep breaths later he'd parked in his usual spot and decided not to think one more time about Christina until he had the answer about Leanne. He could dramatically screech to a halt in the parking lot, say in a firm voice, "Let's go and save her," and embrace the ridiculous "knight" stuff. Who had started that, anyway?

He had a sinking feeling he was responsible for it. Now that it was coming back around to bite him, Brett wished he'd kept his mouth shut.

How often in his life was he going to think that before he finally got the lesson?

At least once more.

No matter how much brainpower he put to the problem of Christina, he couldn't figure her out.

All his life, he'd thought she was hard and tough and looked out for herself above all else.

Why was he learning so late that her exterior was a shield?

She didn't need a knight fighting her battles because she was a warrior herself. For Riley and Parker and Leanne. She'd even been prepared to battle his mother in his defense.

What would it take for her to stand up for herself and what she wanted and deserved?

And what did a man do to make sure he was part of that?

The night he'd come home from Nashville, she'd been human, the kind of woman that made coming home fun. The bat meant it could be dangerous, too, but he had no doubt she'd do whatever it took to protect his kids. Although, she'd already given up more than their mother had in a long time to make sure they were safe and happy.

Instead of looking out for herself, she'd put her job on the line by lugging Parker and Riley into work.

Since Parker could sleep until noon if anyone would let him, Brett knew it hadn't been easy to get them there before sunrise. But she'd done it.

He'd even lost the fear that she was waiting for the perfect window to reunite Leanne and the kids. If he had to guess, he'd say it was the night she'd been prepared to defend Parker and Riley with her life. Anyone who was prepared to put her own safety on the line like that for someone else would be cautious enough not to take silly chances.

Or it could be that he'd finally gotten to know the real Christina. She was smart, too smart to be taken in by manipulation, especially when she was responsible for his kids.

For her own self? She would take the risk with Leanne over and over.

He was on a real roll of terrible Mondays lately. "We could have flirted some, made plans for dinner and let the relationship decision slide for one more evening. But no. She's gotta come out like a honey badger, ready to fight. Like always." Never once had she been easy to get along with. Even at seventeen, she'd been suspicious of him.

That had made it easy to cut her out of his life. He wanted happy and simple, not complicated.

"Why are they so complicated?" Brett muttered as he snatched the bag out of the front seat. "Just one, a nice, easygoing woman. How hard is that to find?"

"For the crazy guy talking to himself?" Macy Gentry said from her place in the doorway. "I'm going to go out on a limb and say difficult."

She held the door open with a smirk. "Even if he's as handsome as you are."

Brett propped his boot on the door and motioned her ahead of him. She rolled her eyes. "I thought you were liberated, sweets.

It's okay to let a woman hold the door for you, what with your hands full and all."

"But I like to hold the door. I like to help people when I can. Why is that such a problem these days?" Brett snapped a second before he realized that was true until it came to Leanne.

Then he held up the coffees in defense when Macy turned on him. She was the glue that kept the reserve rangers in business. No way did he want to be on her bad side. "Sorry. You weren't the target for that."

She snorted. "Well, I guess not." She brushed her blond braid over one shoulder. "And the girl you're courting better not be, either. Why can't *we* like to help without it turning into a federal case? I mean, honestly. Fragile male ego. Not my problem, do you hear me?" She stomped through the lobby and dumped her purse on the metal desk. The clang rattled through the cavernous lobby.

"Who's annoying Macy?" Ash shouted from his office. "Cut it out."

She raised an eyebrow at Brett.

He mumbled, "Sorry."

Instead of telling him where to go, she tipped her head down. "Aw, now, don't look like that. Ain't nothing broken that can't be fixed. You have pie in there?" She peered hard at the bag. "I like pie."

The idea that she might have been stirring the pot in order to maneuver him out of the pie rustled through Brett's brain, but he wasn't going to call her on it. "One for you, one for Ash, but the coffee's mine. I need it. Like air, I gotta have it." He clutched the coffee cups closer.

She patted his shoulder. "Fine compromise. See? You can be flexible and reasonable and all the things people say you aren't. I knew you had it in you."

The criticism, even though it was accurate, stung. Hadn't he learned that lesson? Not to be a self-righteous jerk who shoved his own plans down other people's throats? Smacking his forehead was impossible, but he made a mental note to do it later. Rattling his brain back into the on position was critical.

Ticked off all over again at life, Brett scowled at her. "Know any nice single women? I'd prefer one who doesn't think

I'm a pompous jerk, but I'll work with what I find."

Instead of the expected "Well, there's me, sugar," Macy's expression grew serious. "Um, I thought you already had a handle on the next Missus Hendrix."

"She dumped me." Then he realized he wasn't sure which woman Macy was referring to. "Twice. I've been dumped twice." And left by the woman he'd been married to for a decade.

One day, he'd have to ask himself if the problem wasn't his. Three women, zero love to show for it. The punches were coming from all directions that morning.

Brett swigged his coffee and recalled the flash of Christina's watchful eyes at the diner. It was like she was always waiting for him to…what? What did she expect him to do?

"That was quick and people around town can't figure out what you see in *her*," Macy said with a whistle. "I say you must have messed up big-time, as handsome as you are and you can't keep a girl. It's sad is what it is." She was shaking her head as she walked into the small breakroom off the lobby.

"I didn't do anything except…" His words trailed off because he realized Macy wasn't listening. If he had more energy, he'd follow her, talk about sparks and unreasonable expectations and enough baggage to fill an airplane terminal. He'd explain to her slowly why he hadn't done anything wrong, but that sparks might come later. His teacher in Knoxville had torpedoed his solid plan without giving him any chance to recover and how was that right?

Christina was determined to sacrifice herself for Leanne. That didn't leave a man with much room to maneuver.

Leanne… Listing what he'd done wrong with her could take a month of Sundays.

Even Riley, the little baby girl he'd held in his arms so he could watch every expression that flitted across her face and stared up at the stars with, was unpredictable and scared him with how fast she was changing. With a new haircut almost daily, what would disappear next?

And Macy had stolen his breakfast.

It was no wonder he was exhausted. The women in his life were too much.

It was enough to make a man head for the hills. He needed peace and quiet. Ash's office would have to work.

He held out the cup of coffee. "Macy has your pie. She'll eat it as well as my slice."

Ash grunted. "I'd have let her have it, too. It's the gentlemanly thing to do."

Right. It was also the easy way out, but neither of them was going to acknowledge that.

"How was the training?" Ash asked as he leaned back in his desk chair. "I expected you to be in here yesterday, writing reports and filing them in triplicate."

Brett frowned as he considered that. Should he have done that?

"Fine. I'm prepared to manage for diversity now and I have bonus knowledge in de-escalation techniques. All the requirements of the job have been satisfied."

"For now." Ash took the lid off his cup. "Continuing education. This is going to happen again, you know."

He'd been determined to ignore that. "Day here and there. Should be easy enough." Shouldn't it? Brett sipped his coffee, and then added, "But this trip nearly killed me. I'm not sure I can do both, the job and the family." He met Ash's stare. "You know which one I have to choose if it comes down to it."

His boss nodded. "Sure, but I'm not prepared to give up on you yet. You're smart enough. You can solve this problem." Nothing about his face softened, but Brett understood it was the man, the friend, talking. If Ash was just the boss, Brett's position would be shaky. "How are the kids? Heard a few things over at Smoky Joe's when I was in town this week."

Brett frowned. "They're pretty good. My mom bailed and I had to call in Christina, but it was all…okay." Brett leaned forward. "Wasn't it?"

Ash tangled his fingers together. "Not my place to repeat gossip."

"Except for right now. Tell me." What had happened?

"I ignored tales of Riley smoking in your truck as they sat in the grocery store parking lot." Ash waved a hand. "I'd have to see it to believe it."

Relieved, Brett collapsed against the seat. "I told her the candy cigarettes would come back around. That was a showdown with Riley. Christina's new at this. She thought she could win against a teenage girl, and she almost managed it. Nothing to worry about." Except cavities, but in the big picture, she'd done pretty well for a rookie. "What I don't get is why people automatically assume the worst instead of looking for a reasonable explanation."

Ash's eyes narrowed. "A cop should be more interested in the worst, but I'll chalk up your optimism to being young."

Since he felt roughly two hundred years old that morning, Brett grunted. He knew in his bones he could trust Christina to keep Riley from danger. Why didn't other people give her that same space?

The memory of a laughing Leanne dragging him under the bleachers for his first and last smoke made him pause. Christina had been infamous at Sweetwater High for getting caught breaking into the gym the night before their sophomore year's homecoming game to steal the team's championship trophy. He'd heard two stories. She'd done it either on a dare or because the opposing team had paid her fifty dollars.

Why had he never asked her for the real story?

So Christina and Leanne had made wild decisions as kids, but they would both tell Riley to do as they said and forget what they'd done.

"I trust Christina." Brett was certain of her good motives. He wasn't sure he'd ever felt that way about anyone else, but he would swear in court that he knew her heart.

"Well, now, funny you should mention Christina." Ash sighed. "Are congratulations in order?"

Brett held one finger up as he drained his coffee. The rest of the conversation would require fortification. When he thought he was ready, he braced his hands on the arms of the chair.

Ash shrugged. "Janet seemed…pleased when she waylaid me by the door. She told me she believed a new wife would be the best thing that ever happened to you and the kids. As she said it, three other people who need to get jobs or hobbies argued that

Christina and her *connections* would never mean smooth sailing."

He'd expected anger, but confusion was an old friend. It was his permanent state lately.

"Smooth sailing? In marriage? I watched the pastor of the Methodist church and his wife, two of the nicest, blandest, extremely similar people in this town, argue forcefully over whether they should have spaghetti or lasagna for dinner, right there in the middle of the pasta aisle at the grocery store. People in relationships fight." Brett rubbed his eyes and wished for a nap. He needed to be well rested to deal with any more people. "The engagement story made no sense and still people were desperate to repeat it. Christina and Leanne are tight as sisters. What man in his right mind would divorce one woman, and then marry the other, even a desperate man who is a hair away from losing a job he loves and watching his daughter slowly disintegrate?"

Ash tapped one finger on his desk as he pretended to consider the question. "I get where you're going. On paper, it's a dumb story. Unless it's true."

Listening to the opinions of people in town had always gotten him in trouble. This time, their scandalized gossip should make it easier to walk away from Christina.

"A man crazy in love could decide all that trouble was worth it." Brett tipped his head side to side. "So I hear."

He leaned back to study the ceiling of Ash's office. The wood there was dark and rough. It fit the natural style of the building. It also collected spiderwebs.

"Say a man was that crazy. What would he do?" Brett said slowly.

"Can't say. Never been there myself, but I'd guess a smart man would do almost anything." Ash's calm expression, as if every word out of his mouth was nothing but common sense, settled some of the swirling confusion for Brett.

It did make sense to go after Christina. Finding the person who made his life click, even if on the outside she was the most unlikely puzzle piece, was worth dealing with Sweetwater and coming to terms with their different opinions on what to do for Leanne and smoothing the path for Riley and loving his fearless son the way he was. The woman to tackle that? She'd have to be as confused as he was.

Or mule-headed stubborn as he was. Anything less would fall apart.

"Step one is easy. I have to find Leanne." Brett pulled out his phone. "I'll make some calls to people I worked with in Knoxville. Know anyone on the state police force? We need to check the usual spots. Hospitals, halfway houses and shelters, city and county lockups." He scrolled through his contacts and wondered if he was prepared for whatever answer came.

"Know a guy who works out of Chattanooga. I could see if he has any leads." Ash drummed his hands on his desk, a sure sign he was weighing his words.

"Hit me with it." Brett stood and picked up his hat. "I'm prepared for the worst case." He hoped he was.

"Have you tried calling her?" Ash winced. "Surely you have. I don't have to tell you how to do your job, do I?"

Brett plopped back down in his chair so fast he stirred up a breeze that rustled the papers stacked haphazardly on Ash's desk. "No way it could be that simple. She's been talking to Christina. I know Christina has begged her to come home or for an address. She would drive anywhere to go and get Leanne." He'd barred the kids from calling and he thought his orders might have held this far, but there were people in contact with Leanne. Would she also talk to him?

"Imagine what it would mean if the person you were certain hated you called with a genuine offer to help. Might convince you to do something out of the ordinary, especially if you were scared and alone." Ash checked his empty coffee cup, and then moved to toss it in the trash before shooting a look toward the lobby and setting it back down.

"It can't be that easy, can it?" Brett asked as he stared down at his phone.

"Ash Kingfisher, clearing out blind spots, all day, every day." Ash brushed a hand over his shoulder. "Do not tell Macy I said that."

"Said what?" Macy said from the doorway, a coffeepot in her hand.

"Nothing." Ash brightened. "You made coffee."

"Had to. This one never shares." Macy

pressed a hand to Brett's shoulder. "But I'll go easy on him. Looks like he was flattened by a truck earlier."

"I hear love happens that way," Ash murmured before he sipped his coffee. "Thanks, Mace."

She nodded. "This morning, I was afraid you'd buttoned your uniform too tight, cut off the circulation to your brain. I should have guessed love." She was shaking her head sadly as she left the office.

"Make your calls. Consider calling Leanne first, though. Then do what you need to do and get your head screwed on straight. If you can go after work..." Ash held out both hands. "If not, take a long lunch or whatever. That's on you. Forward the certificate you got for completing that training to me. I want to hand carry it over to the chief ranger, get the guy off my back for a month or two." Ash winced as he stood and braced both hands on the desk as he slowly worked his leg back and forth. "Sitting at a desk is murder on the leg, but still better than running up and down mountains."

Brett ignored Ash's grimace. He knew his boss would try to knock his teeth out if he suggested Ash might need a hand, so he headed for the door. "I'm going out for rounds. Anything I should know? I'll check the reports when I get back in."

"Nah. It was quiet and uneventful around here while you were gone." Ash sighed. "It's almost like you bring the drama with you."

Brett bit back the angry curse that boiled on his lips and strode back out to the car. If he'd had a leg to stand on, he'd have argued.

But Ash was right. His life was a circus with action in too many different rings right now.

Once he was in the peaceful quiet of his SUV, Brett pulled out his phone again. So many times, he'd threatened to remove Leanne's number from his contacts, but there it was. Before he could talk himself out of it in another fit of self-righteous judgment, he punched the number and listened to the rings. After the third one, he realized he'd been holding his breath. When her voice mail picked up, he was annoyed that he wasn't sure what to say. How hard could it be?

"Hey, Leanne, it's Brett." He stared out

the windshield and decided to try humor. "Yes, that Brett. I'm calling because…" Because what? What would make her pick up the phone to call him after she left town to escape him. "I need to talk to you. Please give me a call. It's important." He almost hung up but realized his message might cause her to panic. "The kids are fine. Everybody's well, but they miss you. Please, call me."

As soon as he ended the call, he thought of at least three other things he should have said. "I hope you're well." That would have set a friendly tone. "Christina is okay, too, no thanks to your phone call." That would definitely not set the right tone, but he wanted to say it. If it slipped through his lips, Christina would murder him. That was her battle and she didn't want him fighting it. At least that was getting through his brain.

The thing he definitely should have said yet might have choked on: "I'm sorry." Why did he find it impossible to let that escape his lips? Leanne would have found it impossible not to call back, if only to gloat, if he'd apologized.

And he was sorry. If she was hurt because of his decision to cut off her ties to the kids, words wouldn't fix what was broken.

Instead of calling her back, he texted.

I'm sorry. Yes, that Brett Hendrix. Please call me.

He willed her to answer, and then realized how long he'd been sitting in the parking lot outside the ranger station. Macy was frowning at him from the door, so he waved his phone, then scrolled quickly to find the name of the partner he'd worked with in Knoxville. He'd do the police work he could while he waited to see if the personal touch turned up results.

CHAPTER FOURTEEN

"THANKS FOR LETTING me kill time here, Sharon," Christina said as she wiped down the bar. "I wanted a calming distraction." She glanced around the deserted room. "At this point, it totally fits the bill."

"I swear, three o'clock, it's like somebody calls an all clear and I might as well be the only person left on this planet. The Branch is all well and good in the bright sun at high noon, perfect for cheap meals and plenty of room. At lunch, local movers and shakers are here cutting deals and chewing the fat. Tourists are having their burgers and early happy hours. Even ladies who lunch are happy to spread out and make themselves at home for a couple of hours. They wouldn't be caught here after five when the neon signs come on." She pointed in the general direction of Sweetwater. "Place doesn't pick up again until six and heats up the later it gets. This time of day, mamas and some daddies got a place to be, and then responsibility pushes them back to the real world. Picking up the kids. Getting the groceries. These tourists in here ain't got anywhere to be, but the ol' lizard brain remembers the schedule." She tapped her forehead as if she was wise to the ways of prehistoric thinking patterns that still ruled humans today.

"Nothing surprises you anymore, does it?" Christina asked as she toted the tub of dirty dishes behind the bar.

"Well, now, I wouldn't say that," Sharon said as she eased up on a bar stool. "Didn't expect you to come dragging in today, looking like you'd lost your best friend."

At her choice of words, Christina stumbled and barely managed to lift the tub up onto the counter for the busboy to grab on his way to the kitchen.

"Ah, I see." Sharon propped her chin on her hand. "Tell the old bartender about it, but pour me a root beer first."

"We're on the wrong sides of the bar for this to work, aren't we?" Christina remembered where everything was, and Sharon never changed if she could help it, so it was like slipping right back into the rhythm of the bar to find a chilled glass, plop in a few cubes of ice and fill the mug with a slow fizzing foam.

"I remember when you were behind the bar every night. Those were good days." Sharon sighed as she sipped her drink. "Shame that boy raised such a ruckus and you let him."

"That boy? You mean that father of two who is currently in charge of all the law enforcement rangers at the Smoky Valley Nature Reserve?" Christina braced her hands on the bar and stretched.

"Yeah, him. That was your first mistake, letting him call any shots." She wagged a finger. "When y'all get married, don't let that stand or you will be miserable, I guarantee."

"You fell for that story, too? I don't see how." Sharon knew her as well as most anyone in Sweetwater. She'd worked off and on at the Branch ever since she was old enough to lie about her age in order to wait tables.

"What does that mean? Any woman in this town has a chance of dating one of the town's most eligible bachelors, beat-up as he is, it's you. It'll take a smart woman to handle Brett Hendrix and you're one of the smartest I know." Sharon tapped her glass. "Pour a nice foamy root beer, too.

"What I don't get is why you have the long face now. It's all working out. You and Brett are still young, so you're going to have a rough go of it now and again, but he's pretty enough to make up for that." Sharon raised her eyebrows as if she was waiting for Christina to agree.

She was right. He'd be a pain in the neck for any woman, but there would be plenty of perks to being with Brett Hendrix.

And yet...

"No matter how you look at it, we're too different. Anyone who believes there might be a future for us is deluded." She'd repeated that to herself so many times she was going to start believing it. Soon.

Sharon shifted on the bar stool. "I look at it like this. Ain't nobody ever thought of chocolate and peanut butter and said to themselves, 'Those two things are exactly the same, so let's put 'em together.'" She bent her head closer. "You understand what I'm saying? Sometimes you put things together in new ways and it's sweet and perfect."

Christina had been trying to stop wondering the same thing ever since Leanne's phone call. Whether their differences might mean they were a perfect match. It was easy to daydream a future where Leanne was home and safe, and Christina and Brett were happy together, and it was sweet and perfect.

Finding happiness like that was such a long shot, and she'd never been much of a gambler.

Better to play it safe.

How was she going to make this work? To renew her friendship with Leanne, she'd have to stay away from Brett and manage to do that against his logic and temptation.

Until he found someone new.

Then she'd have to live with bitter jealousy.

But taking what he offered would drive the wedge between her and Leanne deeper, and she was the only person in the world looking out for Leanne.

"How long have you been here, Sharon?" Christina asked.

"Here at the bar today, here running the Branch or here in Sweetwater? Too long. That's the answer to all of them." Sharon chuckled at her cleverness.

"What brought you to town?" Christina wasn't certain what she was looking for with this line of questioning, but she wanted to be on the track to some kind of decision.

"A man. Worked at the reserve after he got out of the military." She stared into the mirror over the bar. "Been gone…nearly twenty years now." She blinked slowly. "Don't seem that long, but it gets away from a person one day at a time." She spread her hands out over the bar. "Took a little inheritance and every bit of retirement to buy this place."

Christina had so many questions but no idea how to ask them.

"So many people think you're lacking the finer feelings, but I'm here to tell you I appreciate your restraint. He died. Car crash, about three years after we got here." Sharon tipped her chin. "So no matter what else happens, it will take place here. For me, this is home. No one's gonna chase me away from home."

Christina straightened up. "What if this is just the place I was born, not my home?" She closed her eyes. "I can wait tables anywhere in this world. What keeps me here, where everyone can name three embarrassing things that I did as a kid and four that I never did but they love to retell. Leanne and I could go somewhere else. Get a fresh start. So many people would like to do that. We could do it."

Sharon narrowed her eyes. "What if it ain't the place holding you back?" She eased off the stool while Christina dealt with a new surge of frustration.

"What if one person could give me an answer?" She pressed the heel of her hand hard against the ache in her head.

"Sorry, life don't work that way." Sharon waved a hand around the Branch. "I stay here because I made the decision that this was home. What I'm saying is that this is all on you, Chris. No one can tell you because you get to choose. Here or there, you make home what it is. You don't like the people here? Next place you live, they'll be the same because people don't change, not unless you give them a reason to."

"Stay or go, makes no difference. Got it." Staring at her clenched fists was the safest decision. Otherwise, Sharon might not appreciate the expression.

"Nah, I'm saying make up your mind and do it. You're the one that determines the success." She shrugged. "Me, given the chance to have everything I wanted right here, I'd plant my feet and refuse to move. You gotta do you."

"It sounds simple when you say it. Why doesn't it feel simple?" Christina asked, stretching her tired shoulder muscles.

"When you consider the whole thing, it's impossible, hon. Break it down into steps. What can you do today to have what you want tomorrow?" She bent closer. "Start where you can."

"Is that what you did, when life…" Fell apart? Disappointed you? Broke your heart?

"Still doing it. Doesn't matter how old you get. Ain't no other path to get through." Sharon raised an eyebrow. "What's the first step?"

That part was easy. "Bring Leanne home. No matter what happened next, there was no other way for her to move on but to make sure Leanne was okay."

Sharon made the "continue" motion with one hand. "Too far ahead."

Christina pulled her phone out of her pocket. "I have to talk to Brett. He's going to get an address." She wasn't sure what else to say to him if he brought up what happened next between them.

But Sharon had given her one of the keys she was missing. "Begin at the beginning. That's where I am."

Sharon smacked her hands on the bar. "You're finally getting it."

The sooner she made it through the first step, the sooner the next step would be clear. Christina desperately wanted that direction.

"I've got to make a phone call." If Brett was no closer to finding Leanne's location, she'd... Well, she had to get the answer first. Then she'd make a plan.

"You might want to go outside for some privacy. Tourists surprise me sometimes, show up when I least expect them. Head through the kitchen. Got a nice smoking spot out in the alley, comfy lawn chair and a view of the backside of the business next door." Sharon made shooing motions. "If you're serious about leaving town, or even if you're not, come back for the dinner crowd. You work for tips. Give the new waitress a good scare, though. She's getting too comfortable around here."

Christina waved at Bill and Blake, the two guys who ran the Branch's kitchen with precision, as she headed out the kitchen door. Before she could push a button on her cell, she saw the reserve SUV parked in front of her truck.

Officer Brett Hendrix was there, staring down at his phone.

CHAPTER FIFTEEN

AFTER HIS SHIFT finally ended, one "misplaced" mountain bike returned to the owner after it was discovered at the Yanu Falls trailhead, Brett was relieved to settle back in the front seat of the reserve's SUV. Ever since his conversation with Ash, he'd done nothing but go over how wrong Christina was for him and vice versa.

So why was he sitting in the parking lot of the Branch, unable to take his eyes off his phone?

None of his calls had turned up a hit on Leanne's whereabouts. Considering he'd focused on an addict's last-chance stops, he was relieved his ex's location was still a question mark.

But he could have been a hero if Leanne had called him back.

And he definitely wanted to be a hero.

He opened his dating app and started

swiping through all his recent matches. "You'd think in a week, the faces might change." But no. He'd already studied all the women in Sweetwater, looking for the right person to fill his heart and his house, and then he'd moved on to this "patented" search that matched people on thirty different personality traits and values.

Why didn't any of them spark any interest?

All he could imagine as he flipped through the profiles was that none of them would wear his fishing cap or dangle her feet in the cold water of the falls. How did he know that? He didn't. The fact that it was unreasonable didn't deter him from being absolutely certain he was right. "None of you would charge up a mountain to go and pick my son up from school." In fact, if he ran a dating show with a big prize to anyone who could start and drive his ragged truck, he had a feeling the show would be canceled due to lack of interest.

Not that it mattered. All he needed was help, not a love match.

Except now that Christina had shown him how much the right woman could bring, not just for Parker and Riley, but also for him, he didn't want to say no to that.

He'd closed his eyes when his phone rang.

The way his breathing sped up as he checked the caller ID was irritating.

But not as irritating as the roll of disappointment that swept over him when he saw his ex-wife's name on the display. Not Christina but the key to getting her what she wanted.

"Hello?" Brett blurted, determined not to miss his chance.

"Hey, Brett," Leanne answered, a shake to her voice that tightened the knot in his stomach. She was nervous. That was never good news. "How are you?"

Brett's lips were a tight line as he stared straight ahead. "Small talk? Is that why you called? We were never all that good at it."

The crackle of the line sounded more like a landline than a cell, and Brett listened hard to pick up any clues from the background noise. It almost had the clink and murmur of a crowded restaurant.

Or a busy waiting room, somewhere

where lots of people were crammed in a small space.

"Are you hurt?" Brett straightened in his seat. If this was the opportunity he and Chris were waiting for, he'd run inside and grab her and they'd...

Leave his kids all alone for who knew how long.

"No, I'm well." Leanne cleared her throat. "Thank you for asking."

Brett pulled the phone away to study the display. Yes, it was Leanne's number.

Demanding to know where she'd been for a month would make him seem impatient and judgmental and too much like the old self he was trying to leave behind.

Better to try a request.

"Please come back to Sweetwater." Brett cleared his throat to eliminate the gruff tone and asked, "What do you need, Leanne? Tell me. I'll get it for you. Whatever it is."

This time the silence was filled with the sounds of a muted conversation.

He had no idea where she might be.

"A favor. A big favor." She cleared her throat.

Bail money and a ride home. That had to be it. How much trouble was she in?

"I'm going to text you an address. Could you meet me there tomorrow at two? Dress nice, not like a tuxedo or even a suit, and definitely not in the park ranger uniform." Her breathless tumble of words came to a sudden halt and Brett replayed them in his mind.

"What's this about, Leanne?" He couldn't even build an off-the-wall theory for all of those words to be arranged in that manner.

"Please, if you love me... No, never mind that. I know better than that." She cleared her throat again. "Because you love Parker and Riley and they love me, please meet me there. You could bring them if you want to."

Surely they weren't talking about jail, then. Even Leanne wouldn't be that selfish. *Would she?*

"What about Christina? Are you telling her wherever you've been hiding for the past month? Because I won't be bringing the kids so—"

"You'll be asking her to watch them," Leanne finished his sentence. "No. I don't want to see Christina. And I'm not going to get angry that you won't be bringing Parker and Riley. Tomorrow is about you and me, anyway. I'll need more time for them."

Brett wasn't sure why he'd say it, but he'd call her tone of voice sad. Of all the people in her life, his kids loved her the most.

"Can I count on you?" She laughed. "What am I saying? Of course I can count on you. You might never have loved me, but you'd never let me down if you could help it." Leanne sounded a bit like her old self, carelessly breezy but with an undertone of anger that never seemed to fade when she talked to him. What was this all about?

"I'll see you tomorrow, Brett." Her voice was so soft that it took him a minute to realize that she'd ended the call. An address in Sevierville popped up on his phone screen.

He'd never forced out the apology, either. Would blowing his chance to make huge progress between the two of them come back to bite him?

He dropped the phone in the passenger

seat and tightened both hands on the steering wheel.

A smart man would never have agreed to attend this—whatever it was—without more information.

He would also start the SUV up and pull out of the parking lot instead of getting out to walk over to talk to the woman glaring at him from the doorway to the Branch's kitchen.

"Loitering is against the law, Officer." Christina crossed her arms over her chest. "Do I need to call the cops?"

Brett pulled his hat off and ran a hand through his hair. When she watched every move he made with a suspicious but interested gaze, he wondered if there was a way around all their troubles and back to being more than friends. That was the only thing that would be enough for him.

"What do you want?" she asked, and pointed to the center of her chest. "We know what I want. Do you have an address?" Every word was tightly controlled.

I want your smile.

I want another kiss.

More than anything, I want this tangled relationship unknotted so that we can...

That was the problem. He didn't know how to finish that sentence, and until he could find the answer, she deserved some space.

That was the only thing he didn't want to give her.

This wild-goose chase of Leanne's could solve at least part of their problems. He'd bring Leanne home and make an effort to repair her connection to his kids. For Parker's and Riley's sakes.

And Christina's if he was being honest.

He did understand loving someone who didn't deserve it. He'd lived his whole life doing the same thing. First step: figure out Leanne's problem.

"I have a lead, but I came to ask a favor. Can you stay with Parker and Riley tomorrow? I'm not sure when I'll be back, but you won't have to stay overnight. By the time I make it home, I'll have an address for you. I swear." He waved his hat at the Branch's kitchen window, where they had a steady, growing audience. Then he noticed Sweetwater Souvenir, the town's newest shop, was kitty-corner from the Branch, and Janet Abernathy and Regina Blackburn were watching the whole conversation. Arms crossed. He couldn't see their expressions, but he understood that they were watching him. Suspiciously. Not Christina.

"I'll be gone for the afternoon, though. If you're working out at the campground, they could come with you." He stared hard at the Branch door and considered explaining to her that they couldn't come with her there.

Then he remembered his meltdown when he'd realized Leanne was hanging out there.

He didn't have to explain anything to her about the Branch. "You know that, don't you? I don't want you to miss work."

He realized how lame he sounded a second after the last word formed on his lips. She worked too hard. Here he was telling her she could continue to do her job and the favor he needed, too. What a charming guy. As soon as he saw the fire light in her eyes, he clapped his hat back on his head. "I'm sorry. I'm going to stop digging now. I'll text you the time."

He turned on a heel to march his way out of trouble, but she stopped him. "I almost think you're capable of learning new things, and then…" He turned as she waved a hand in an "you do this kind of stupid stuff" manner.

"You gotta admit that it's easier for me to admit when I'm wrong now." He winced. "I've done it enough lately."

Her lips were twitching as she stepped back. "Guess I better improve my forgiving skills."

"I'd ask if you thought we could ever be friends, I mean, after I gain a lick of common sense." He enjoyed how her cheeks colored. "It's funny because it's true."

"But you aren't asking," she said as she propped both hands on her hips. "Smart. Also very you."

"I know who stands between us. We do this in stages. Leanne is the most important, first step." As he said it, he realized he meant it. She shot him a sideways glance before staring out over Sweetwater's busy main street, which convinced him he was on the right track. Whatever had caused the cooling between them, it was connected to Leanne. "And I understand."

She nodded and wrapped her arms around herself, smaller all of a sudden than she'd been when she'd been preparing to confront him. "Well, that's it, then."

Brett twirled the hat on his finger, and then remembered his audience. Rangers did not twirl the official hat of the park uniform. "Maybe. Maybe not."

Christina bit her lip. Brett wondered what she wanted to say. He hated that there was anything she might not feel free to express, but he had no one to blame other than himself.

"I've got to get the kids. We're making a french fry run on the way home from school today. Bribery works." He held up a hand to stall her words. She was going to throw his lecture about nutrition back in his face and he deserved it. "The kid loves them. He aced his math test. And we all have to live a little. A wise philosopher told me that once."

Christina rolled her eyes as she stepped back up onto the sidewalk. "Don't hang around in the parking lot. It gives me the willies. Next time, have a seat at the counter. I'm buying." Then she tossed him a smile before returning inside.

Occasionally for the rest of the short afternoon and evening, he'd remember that smile. It wasn't a yes, but it wasn't a no. Why did that feel like such a victory?

If he thought for too long about their problems, their history of friction and the explosive spark Leanne would always be between them, no matter their relationship, Brett could convince himself that being smart was the best answer.

Then he'd remember that smile… While his kids shouted about who got to hold the remote control, or in the middle of Sweetwater's rush-hour traffic jam at the stoplight to the highway.

And when he should have been sleeping.

That smile would pop back up in his memory.

BY THE TIME he'd gotten the kids to school the next day and worked through half a shift, he was sleep deprived and ready to get on to the next step in his plan to get his life back.

As he pulled up in front of a nondescript office building in Sevierville, Brett double-checked the address Leanne had texted.

At home, the most important people in his world were unaware that life was about to change. Christina had accepted his promise without complaint or suspicion or anger. They trusted him. This secret meeting seemed to counter that trust.

Guilt over leaving without telling any of them where he was going had turned his stomach into a hard knot, but the list of all the ways Leanne could be in trouble… Well, if he could spare the people he loved the pain of that, he would do it.

He watched an older couple slide out of a large sedan. They might have been headed into church dressed as they were. "Nice clothes," he muttered under his breath, still annoyed at Leanne's advice because it reminded him of other times and so many arguments. He dressed how he dressed. Because he was an adult. Today that meant khakis and a button-down, and if that wasn't good enough…

Annoyed at himself now for letting her get in his head as she always did, Brett said, "Excuse me. Are you here for a meeting at two?"

The older guy raised his eyebrows. "Meeting. Like a twelve-step meeting?" He glanced at his wife. "Not rightly sure, but I expect they handle that when we aren't around." He nodded his head side to side as if he was weighing the possibilities. "Is there a support group for families and friends? Maybe there's some kind of gathering for them we don't know about because we live over near Johnson City. Can't make the trip weekly." As the man shoved his hands in his pockets and considered his answer to what had seemed like a pretty straightforward question to Brett, presumably his wife leaned over and whispered something in his ear.

Then the old guy waved both hands. "What am I saying? This is a ceremony. Graduation. No stepping today. We're gonna party and celebrate and let them work through the steps tomorrow, you know?"

His wife wrapped her hand around his arm. "We should know. This is our second graduation."

"Graduation." Brett repeated it slowly as he put the pieces together.

"From this treatment program. It's the last day. Everyone's going home, so it is a kind of celebration." She smiled up at Brett. "Easy enough to have doubts, isn't it? But if you love them, you have hope this time is the one that works. Addiction is powerful. Only hope can stand up to that."

Stopped in his tracks, Brett watched them disappear inside. Shock made it impossible to catch the door as it shut, so he leaned slowly against the brick instead of following them in.

Treatment. Leanne had left town to seek treatment for her problem. All alone.

Instead of a tearful, dramatic display of hurt feelings and desperate need, she'd left in the middle of the night and taken herself to get the help he'd begged her to when he'd discovered how bad her addiction was.

Then she'd insisted it wasn't a problem and she could quit whenever she wanted.

Watching her do it had nearly killed them both. Riley had been young enough that all she knew was that things were not right. She'd clung to both of them. If there'd been any key to Leanne's first battle win, it had been Riley.

What an idiot he'd been to remove the only things Leanne would fight for from her life.

And how strong his ex-wife had to be to decide to fight. There'd been no grand announcements or threats, or even what could have been a reasonable request for encouragement. Leanne had done this all on her own.

And of all the people she could share this announcement and celebration with, she'd only invited him.

Not Christina, her oldest friend and the one who'd lifted her out of a hundred different messes.

What did that mean?

"You're going to have to go inside to find out," Brett muttered. "And you should have worn a tie."

Brett straightened up, smoothed his hand over his shirt and ran it through his hair, then reached for the door. He'd spent a lifetime pretending to be in total control. He could do it here, too.

Instead of a large auditorium with a

stage in front, he came to a narrow hallway. A sign with a bright red arrow pointed him down to a single open door that led into a small gymnasium. There were no rows of seats facing a podium, but a large circle dominated the center of the room. A few chairs lined the walls. He could see the wife of the couple he'd met outside seated there, but the older guy was inside the circle next to a middle-aged man who looked like he'd been to war and back and had barely survived. It was easy to assume he knew the younger guy's story, but the older guy, the one who must be his father, clasped his son's hand tightly, suggesting nothing in his history mattered. There were two people in the world who loved him so much that they'd show up for him again and again and hope it was the time that worked.

They loved him. They would hope for him until they were gone from this world.

How awesome it was to have that kind of love.

Brett wasn't sure he'd ever experienced it until Riley was born, but now, no matter what happened, he'd love his kids in that manner.

Then he saw Leanne. She was perched on the edge of her seat, nervously swinging one foot. As always, she was the most beautiful woman in the room, but instead of drawing men like moths to a flame, she was chewing one fingernail and staring hard at her phone. He could tell the minute she realized he was there. She went perfectly still. She didn't smile or do any over-the-top Leanne thing. She waited.

It was easy to see where he was supposed to sit. The circle would be complete as soon as he took the chair next to Leanne. And she needed him.

Brett moved to his seat, braced for whatever tactic she chose to begin the conversation.

"I wasn't sure you'd come. Expected a text about work or whatever." Leanne tried a smile, but it faded quickly. "Thank you."

Caught off guard at how easy it was to settle in next to her, Brett clasped his hands together. "I've turned over a new leaf. Instead of being obnoxiously righteous so that people wish I would catch on fire, I'm going to…not do that. Anymore."

Leanne's eyebrows were raised to her

hairline as she laughed. "I didn't expect that."

"Me, either." Brett grunted a laugh. "It's a real day of surprises."

She started to say something else, but the woman running the show, one wearing an official white coat to show that she was indeed a doctor even though she was young enough to still be studying in the quad, stood and moved to the center.

"Thank you, everyone, for coming. At New Beginnings, we feel it's important to have a ceremony that marks the end of treatment. Some people call it a graduation, but to me, it's more of a commitment." She moved in a slow circle, her eyes falling steadily on each person seated there. "Today, you're going to leave the safety of treatment and head back out into the world. That world hasn't changed, so unless you have, unless you've done the work and made a difference inside, you'll continue to struggle."

Leanne shifted in her seat, distracting Brett, so he glanced around the circle. There were all ages represented, both male and female.

"We asked you to have an accountability partner join you in this last circle. This is the person who will help you with all the work left to do." The woman continued to slowly pace the circle. "To each of *you*, you aren't here because the person next to you loves you the most or the least, or because you know them the best or the least. They've chosen you because you can be counted on to give them the truth. To watch them and listen to them and not turn away because it's too difficult to be honest. I hope you're here because you've proved your loyalty and your toughness, because this is a hard battle and they need support."

Brett studied Leanne's face, but she didn't turn toward him. He could understand that. He'd failed on that front more than once. In the early days, he hadn't wanted to believe she had a problem. Then, when it became too bad to pretend, he'd had zero trouble giving her enough truth to choke on.

"Before you agree, each person in the circle has something to say. We can't ask for amends in this single conversation, but we can clear the air and commit to going forward." She stopped in front of the guy and his father. "Leon, you start us off."

Brett wasn't sure what he'd been prepared for that day, but he'd expected to be highly annoyed by the time it was done. Instead, his heart was broken over and over and over by the stories he heard around the circle. Leon looked like he'd been through a war because he had. An actual war in Iraq and Afghanistan that had left him with PTSD and a drug problem that had destroyed his life after his military service. He wanted a fresh start. That was the common heartbreaking request. Everyone there wanted to begin again.

When it came to his turn with Leanne, he was prepared but so raw emotionally that he would have agreed to anything she asked.

"When they asked each of us to invite the person who could stand by our side in the world, all I saw was your face." Leanne finally turned to him. She didn't reach out to take his hands, but her containment was so unlike her that Brett was certain she was going through something new. "I don't deserve your help, Brett. I know it. We're locked in this…relationship because of my own scheming or whatever." She shrugged a shoulder, and he understood perfectly. It was hard to categorize what they had, but it meant a lot to both of them because of Parker and Riley. "I apologize." Tears spilled down her cheeks and she brushed them away angrily. "I don't want to start all over, but I want to start fresh. Even if we were never in love, I love my kids and I want to be in their lives and you did exactly what they needed when you told me not to see them anymore. I was playing with fire that would burn down everything. That brought me here. The threat of never seeing my kids is rock bottom like I never imagined. So, thank you. And then you showed up for me. Again. Like you always do. Because you're you."

Brett watched the tears spill down her cheeks and wished he was the kind of guy who had a handkerchief.

"Will you help me? Will you give me truth when I need it and grace to start over?" Leanne met his stare. The hardness he'd seen in her eyes glittered like broken glass. It was easy to see how much his answer mattered to her.

"I will. Riley and Parker need you." He pried open her hand and squeezed it tightly, mad at himself again for being so unbending that she'd ever doubted his support and relieved to the point of weakness that he hadn't blown off her request. "There are people in Sweetwater who need you. I'll do whatever I can to make sure you stay true to this moment."

This wasn't about being her knight, either. This wasn't fighting battles for her. This was standing behind her, ready to catch her if she fell. That was what Leanne needed. And Christina.

And his beautiful daughter. Crashing realization while a roomful of people looked on was a new experience.

Leanne's shaky nod was her only answer and they both turned back to the doctor, who continued around the circle.

As the minutes ticked by, the mood in the room lifted. Instead of tense expectation, there was a lighter, more celebratory vibe. Leanne hadn't been the only one in the room uncertain of the answer she'd get.

Brett was mentally energized but physically worn-out to be so relieved. He'd expected the worst. Instead, Leanne had presented him with the very best. She'd made the decision for herself. As he understood addiction, that was the only way this would ever work.

They waited patiently for photos and presentation of certificates. There was a sheet cake to eat and terrible punch to drink and the sun was setting by the time he and Leanne were standing on the sidewalk outside. He raised a hand to wave at Leon and his parents as they got in their car.

"Nothing like baring your feelings in front of perfect strangers to make new friends," Leanne said as she smiled up at him.

"Sure. Does it do anything to make two people who fought like cats and dogs into friends?" Brett asked. He had a feeling it did. If she was ready to make a change, he owed it to her, to Christina and, most of all, to his kids to make it happen, whatever it took.

"I hope so. I'm still processing that you showed up for me."

"I didn't wear a tie. I should have." Brett tugged on his sleeve and brushed at a wrinkle. "All I could hear was all the times—"

"I nagged about how you dressed." Leanne nodded. "You are bad at picking wives. Your first one was a total mess." She bumped his shoulder with hers. "You deserve the best the next time around."

Since she'd stepped pretty close to the nagging doubt that had bothered him ever since he'd realized what his role was in her recovery, and he'd promised her the truth, Brett decided he couldn't back away. "You aren't thinking that will be you, are you?" He squeezed his nape, feeling like he was dangling off a skyscraper. He didn't want to hurt her, especially not now, but she shouldn't go any further with making plans for them. In no universe did they work. He'd already given up years and so much energy proving that time and time again.

Her eyes were wide as her mouth dropped open. "No, I'm not pining for you, Brett. You don't have to worry about that. I've schemed enough to bring us together. Now I'm going to…" She stared out over the parking lot, where Christina's old car was parked in the shade. "First, I'm going to make amends. Then I'm going to figure out what I want. I'm not sure it's in Sweetwater."

The unease that settled over his shoulders surprised him. He might not love her like either of them wanted for a marriage, but he was worried about her. "But not Knoxville." That had been where their lives imploded. Surely she wasn't planning to go back there. She immediately shook her head in response and it was reassuring.

"No way. Gatlinburg. Or Pigeon Forge. Cherokee if I have to in order to find work. My boss at the Christmas store told me he couldn't hold my job, but I'll go back to make sure. I did good there. I'm thinking I need to be close enough to spend time with my kids, but far enough away from Sweetwater that there isn't an interested citizen at every corner waiting for my next scandalous act." Leanne crossed her arms over her chest. "That could be all right, don't you think?"

The fact that she'd given any thought to what she needed to be successful was another sign that something was changing in

Leanne. Those adjustments were reasons to be hopeful. He'd encourage them, support them and do his best to make each one happen. "Both places have about a million shops. You'll find something fast. I can see this working."

Leanne nodded once. "Yep. I'll get more than one job. I want stability and I want it soon. I'm ready to work hard to get it."

There and then, Brett resolved to help her find the right job. No one needed to work three part-time jobs to make the rent, and he didn't want that for Leanne. Christina was working before sunup and long after sundown. That was temporary. Work like that would wear her down quickly. Leanne needed good work and plenty of time with her kids. Maybe he could find her an office job—work with regular hours. Had she even considered something full-time?

Then he realized he was doing what he always did. He was preparing to take over.

"I'll make some calls to people I know, to see if they've heard of any jobs, if you'd like that?" Brett smiled at how her eyebrows rose. "I'm making offers now, not giving orders. Retail would be good for you, but a nine-to-five would be easier. That's all."

She studied his face. "All these changes. What's causing them?" Then her face fell. "Christina. Are you telling me it's Christina?"

That was hard to answer. "I'm not sure and I don't want to talk about my feelings in this parking lot. Are you coming back to Sweetwater tonight? Let's ride together."

She exhaled slowly. "All the thinking I've been doing, and that's the answer I can't find. I want to. I want to see Riley and Parker, but I don't need to be crashing on your couch. Christina and I…" She crossed her arms over her chest, hands clenched tightly. "I just… The thought of the two of you together, I'm not there yet."

Brett jingled his keys. "We aren't together. Does that help?" He clicked the locks open on his SUV. "If you want to patch things over with Christina, you need to do it in person. If you need a place to stay, I'll float you a loan for a hotel room." He could do it. That was the missing piece that made this decision easier and he wanted to do it. "Tomorrow we can start again, tackle talking with the kids about where you've been and what it means going forward. Then, if you need to sleep on the couch, you can. Christina said it was the most comfortable couch she'd ever crashed on."

Leanne rolled her eyes. "She sleeps on her own couch every night. I guess she should know." She turned toward Christina's car.

"We'll come back for it tomorrow." Brett wasn't sure why he was pushing. She needed to be independent and she should be returning Christina's car as quickly as possible with a huge, flowery apology instead of a grudging frown.

Whatever might happen with Christina in the future, they had to get over this breakup first, the one between best friends who'd had each other's backs since the trailer park. He didn't have much to do with it, but he could do what he could.

"Fine. I'll ride with you. I guess she's at your house now. With my kids." Leanne yanked open the door and slid inside.

Brett counted to twenty just as he had when they were married. It still didn't lessen his anger any, but he might have been a bit calmer as he got behind the wheel. "Keeping them safe. When everyone else disappeared, she stepped in and she's done so much. Whatever you think has happened, get that right."

Leanne was silent as he maneuvered the city streets and then hit the two-lane highway back to Sweetwater.

"I can't believe she kissed you. It's like…" She shook her head. "When we were kids, she had this massive crush on you, but she would never do anything about it. Do you think she's been holding a grudge or…secretly wishing to have you for herself all these years?"

Brett blinked slowly as he did his best to keep the SUV between the lines, then he laughed so loud and so long that Leanne was concerned and he wasn't too sure he hadn't experienced a meltdown himself. "A crush? On me." He gasped for air. "Wishing? For me." He wiped the tears away and shook his head. "I do not think that. At all. Even if what you say is true, I have a feeling the first year you and I were married I fixed any lingering feelings in a New York minute. Killed them dead."

Leanne studied his face. "You were so bossy as a kid, always telling us how to act and ways to care for Riley and just…"

"Sucking the joy out of life at every turn. Yeah, that's how I remember it, too. I was determined to do better than my parents ever did, and I knew that the whole thing was going to be on my shoulders, so I had better take control."

He gripped the steering wheel tighter as they rolled into Sweetwater. The story of Leanne riding shotgun would make the rounds quickly.

Good. If he'd been the poster boy for being right before, he could change his reputation. Being right was nice, but being compassionate was better. If he'd focus on that, his life would be better, too.

"We were so young. It's a miracle we made it out in one piece and the kids did, too," Brett said.

"Not sure it was a miracle. I do think you're the only one that got us through." Leanne squeezed his forearm. "And I never appreciated it until now."

"Remember that time Christina was staying over to help with Parker and I got up in the middle of the night to tell you to keep it down." Brett was embarrassed at the memory, but for some reason, it had been playing on a constant loop. Christina and Leanne were the kind of friends who made it for a lifetime. He had no business coming between them, then or now.

And even as a girl, Christina had been the one to respond when they needed her.

"All along, she's been the kind of person who steps in to lend a hand. I was an idiot to push her out." Brett glanced over at Leanne. "I thought she enabled you. Why I couldn't see that I was doing the same thing..."

"My whole life, she's been the only person I could count on." Leanne held up a hand. "I mean, you could be relied on, but with her, I could show her the worst and she'd still love me like a sister, like family even though there's nothing but time tying us together."

"All I could see was the heartbreaker," Brett muttered, "and she's been better than both of us. Giving. Patient. She didn't

punch me in the nose for my superiority."
It was maddening to be confronted with,
over and over again, how dumb he'd been
because he was so certain of his judgment.
"Don't throw away a friend like that, Lee."

She wrinkled her nose. "No man is
worth that, huh? Not even the upstanding
Brett Hendrix, hero of Sweetwater High
and the Smoky Valley Nature Reserve and
a little ranch house on White Oak Lane."

As he slowed down to turn into the
driveway of that very house, Brett had to
come to terms with how much he'd loved
that, being treated like a hero by the town
of Sweetwater. Marrying the bad girl had
given that myth an early boost. Persevering
and winning their divorce case had only
confirmed what most of the town thought.
He was a good man.

But all his life, he'd been determined to
become what people said he was. Now that
he knew how far off he'd been, what was
he going to do about it?

"We're going to draw up a new agreement, Lee." It made so much sense. His
life had fallen apart the second he'd cut
her out of the kids' lives. "As long as you

stay clean, we're going to share custody. As soon as you have a place." He nodded and watched her question die on her lips. She was thinking ahead, planning for her kids.

And he had to live like this treatment was going to be the answer she needed.

"I want that, Brett," Leanne said softly, "eventually. More than anything, I want Riley and Parker to be safe and happy, though. Above all else, you see to that. You and I are going to argue, but I trust you to keep the most important things in my life safe and sound." She nodded firmly. "I'm not dumb enough to think one stint in treatment will cure my problems, but I have something to fight for. Thank you for the second chance."

Brett thought about correcting her. This wasn't their second chance. He'd lost track of what number they were on, but in the end, it didn't matter. This was the important one. They were tied together and it was in his best interest to help her succeed.

He turned off the engine and watched her hands clench together.

"Are you ready to do this?" Brett asked. He could imagine the celebration that

Parker and Riley would throw when she walked through the door.

"Making amends is a big part of recovery. I started with you because I thought you would be the easiest to talk to." Her laugh was so much like the carefree girl she'd been that it was impossible not to join in.

"Imagine that. Me, the easy one."

"Yeah." Leanne studied the front door. "Christina… I was so angry at her when I heard you guys were getting married."

"It was a misunderstanding." Brett sighed. "I was looking for a wife, though. Somebody sweet and easy to get along with, a woman who could love Parker and Riley and give me a chance to breathe easily. Thought I'd found her, a sweet schoolteacher from Knoxville, but she wanted more than that." He snorted. "Another example of me trying to control the world. All my life, all I dreamed of was a better family than mine. I'm still looking. I don't know. I have learned it's going to cause trouble if I'm only focused on the help I need, not what she wants."

Leanne was watching him when he

turned to look at her. "You don't usually change your mind once it's made up, Brett. What's causing the hesitation?"

Was he going to say it aloud? The recent memory of his promise to give her nothing but the truth was right there. He couldn't easily ignore it.

"I've spent too much time with Christina." His words were loud in the quiet cab. "When I consider all my potential match-ups, no one measures up to her."

"Oh man." Leanne covered her face with both hands and Brett was uncertain what to do.

"Christina's not going to go for anything between us." Brett knew it was the truth. It had taken a long time, but he was see-ing the real Christina now. He'd thought she was a seductress and hard, but she was careful and contained and loyal beyond all else. Following her around and insisting on pursuing what he wanted above her desire would be falling back into his old patterns. Everyone was going to make a fresh start, even the head control freak in charge.

"Because of me. After all I've done, she'd turn her back on a man who could love her the way she deserves." Leanne shook her head. "I was not prepared for this level of amends. All our lives, she's been the one to give. I'm not ready for the tables to be turned like this."

Brett propped his arm on the door and covered his eyes. The whole situation was impossible. "You don't have to worry, Lee. There's not much between us and I can take no for an answer. We're all going to be okay on the other side of this, so just…get your friend back. We'll do family dinners and you and Christina can have sleepovers at her run-down cabin while I drive by without you knowing because I have to keep an eye out, and then when you get an apartment in Gatlinburg or wherever, Riley and Parker will come and swim on Saturdays and you and Christina can work on your tans, then go out to eat and to the movies and be happy. If you can ever convince her to take a day off because she works all the time." Brett scoffed. "What I mean to say is that none of this is the end of the world."

Leanne didn't answer immediately. "I'm going to do something I hate." She nodded firmly. "But it's the right thing. It's late. I want plenty of time for what comes next. Could you take me to the most expensive hotel you know of and pay for the best room they have?" Her lips were twitching. "You did offer, after all."

Brett chuckled and started the SUV. "I did. I will. And in the morning, we can go pick up Christina's car. Then we're going to get to work."

She offered him her hand to shake. "I'll be ready."

CHAPTER SIXTEEN

WHEN BRETT TEXTED her that he was going to be later than he expected, Christina didn't worry. That had to mean he was close to finding Leanne and she'd have the answer she needed soon enough. She'd gone back to dancing with Parker, who still managed to beat her every time they played the video game with all the hip-hop moves.

She'd tempted Riley into baking chocolate chip cookies with her by promising one of her mother's family recipes. It came straight from the back of the bag of chocolate chips. Since Riley had never believed her in the first place, it was easy to get a laugh out of the kid when she produced the bag with a dramatic "ta-da" flourish.

"How has school been this week? You and Naya still bitter enemies?" Christina asked as she tossed a handful of chocolate chips in her mouth. Riley opened wide and pointed, so Christina closed one eye for better focus, took careful aim and landed a three-point shot from the other side of the island. Riley chewed and raised her hands in victory.

Clearly, to win this one over, she was going to need sugar. Lots of sugar.

Riley bent to peek in the oven. "I don't know what we are. I blocked her number and we haven't spoken to each other on the bus." She scooted up to sit on the island.

"And you're okay with that?" Christina asked casually as she washed the mixing bowl.

"Is this going to be an after-school special?" Riley grabbed a few of the remaining walnuts and put one in her mouth. "It's okay. I have other friends."

"Good. That's good." Christina wanted both of the Hendrix kids to have plenty of support forever and ever. Then they didn't have to cling so hard to the people who might not be great for them.

"Is Daddy bringing us home a new mommy?" Riley wagged her head from side to side. "Or the old mommy, I guess?" Her expression was almost blank, but something around her eyes convinced Christina that lying to pretend she had no idea what was going on would be a betrayal.

And Riley didn't need that in her life.

Christina checked around the corner to see that Parker was glued to his television show.

Then she stepped closer to Riley. "I hope so. I think so, but if your father comes home and Leanne's not with him, can you—"

"I can play it cool, Aunt Chris. For Parker." She met Christina's stare directly, too wise for her years already. "You can count on me. I want to know what's going on."

Christina wrapped her arms around Riley in a surprise hug, ignored her squawk and whispered, "I get it. Me, too."

Instead of pushing her away, Riley tentatively touched Christina's shoulders. "You're going about the whole wicked stepmother thing all wrong, you know. I guess making me like you is part of your evil plan, but then what?"

The girl's lips were twitching as she squirmed backward.

"I'm going for evil aunt, not stepmother.

There are fewer role models, you know? We may have to work our way through it." Christina started putting away the dishes, determined not to get into the plans for her life with a teenager.

Even if she might appreciate any input.

"It's not because of me, is it?" Riley hopped down from the counter. "Because you could give us another shot. Once Mom's home, I can ease up. My dad... He's so harsh sometimes. Only with her, but somebody needs to defend her. That's me. But he's pretty into you, Chris. That fishing trip..." She rolled her eyes. "So much flirting."

"What do you know about flirting?" Brett said from the doorway, Parker clinging to his right leg like he could scale it. "Did you miss all the shouting?"

"Dad's home! Dad's home! Dad's home!" Parker jumped up and down every time he said it until everyone had clapped hands over their ears. Brett finally pressed a hand to Parker's head, and then said, "In case the neighbors missed it, we're all in the loop now."

"Christina let me wait until you got here,

instead of making me go to bed." Parker held both arms up in the air, mirroring his big sister. "I'm the *winner*!"

"And now it's time for bed." Riley held up both hands like claws. "First one to the toothpaste picks the book. I've been missing my princesses." Then she feinted left and right to convince Parker to run.

"Never!" he screamed, and sprinted toward the bedroom.

Before she left, Riley glanced over her shoulder at Christina. She nodded and followed Parker.

The silence in the kitchen was heavy.

"I want to be prepared for the worst, but I'm so tired of imagining it. Where is she?" Christina asked.

"Tonight, she's staying over in the fancy hotel near the interstate, thanks to my credit card." Brett was rolling his sleeves up as he walked slowly closer. "And tomorrow, she'll be here to see Riley and Parker. You? She's still...trying to figure out you."

"But her ex-husband she's on good terms with." Christina rubbed her forehead as she considered what that might mean. Had the world turned upside down at some point when she wasn't looking? "And you—" She waved a hand. "You dressed up to go and track her down?"

Wouldn't a uniform have gotten him more answers?

"Actually, she invited me to a ceremony." He wrapped his hands around her arms and it was impossible to ignore how much steadier she felt with his skin on hers. "She left town to check into a treatment facility. The alcohol… She thought she could handle it, that it was different. But it wasn't, not for her. I pushed her out of town, and I'm sorry. I apologized to her and I'll give you another one. Leanne needed someone to hold her accountable. She picked me. I'm asking you to do the same for me. I'll repeat the request in front of the kids and Leanne, but I need someone to call me on my…" Brett stared down at the floor as if he was searching for the right word.

"Pigheadedness." Christina nodded. "Or hypocrisy." He clutched a hand over his heart. "Or something that means 'total lack of compassion for someone struggling against a real sickness.' Do you know the word for that?"

He grimaced. "Being a total Brett?"

She didn't want to, but it was impossible not to chuckle. That was the trouble with handsome men. They could always charm themselves out of trouble.

"I kept my promise. We know where Leanne is and she's healthy, maybe in better shape than I've seen her in years." Brett stepped closer, his chest within easy leaning distance. "Is it time to figure out us?"

"You're certain there is an us?" Christina asked, unsure of what she wanted for the rest of her life but crystal clear on what she needed in the next minute. She'd missed him. How long had it been? They could still measure it in hours, not even days, but she didn't want to go without Brett Hendrix and his kooky, sweet kids in her life for even a second.

"I'm not, because I understand your fears. And if you tell me that this is not the right time for us to build a relationship, I won't push. I might wait and ask again in a month, but I'll take your answer, even if I don't like it." He winced. "Adulting is the worst, am I right?"

"Now who sounds like Riley?" Christina

said. "She told me I was messing up the evil stepmother bit. Because I'm so awesome, obviously."

"Obviously." Brett's smile at this close range was devastating, but she couldn't look away. "Did you get the idea she might be in the market for said stepmother? And that she was sizing you up for the uniform?"

There was no correct way to answer that.

"We know Parker is in. Three out of four Hendrixes agree. That's nearly as good as the dentists, so now we turn our attention to how to fix what's broken between you and Leanne, now that we know she's safe."

He made a good point. She'd checked herself into rehab. Instead of running wild, she'd done something to save herself. It was time to build on that.

"A job and a place to stay. Leanne already knows what her next steps are. I say we help her complete it, and then…" Brett stared into her eyes, the corner of his mouth tipped up. "Then we circle back to the question you haven't answered yet."

"No circling back." Christina pressed her hand over the crisp dress shirt he'd worn on his secret mission. "You know how sometimes nothing is coming together but you keep sifting through stuff until you eventually find the one thing that makes everything click?" He pursed his lips and was half a second from making a smart remark. She'd learned to read that in his eyes. "You're going to need to get better at a heart-to-heart conversation. Try practicing."

Brett blinked innocently. "Go on."

"Good start." Christina knew it was going to come out in a jumble.

She also knew Brett would get it.

"I thought I had no friends here. The only one I had left me stranded. But Woody stepped up. Janet and Luisa helped me make it through single parenting for the first time. And Sharon gave me a huge piece of advice. I'm still chewing it up into smaller pieces so I can swallow it." Brett opened his mouth but closed it with a snap when she tilted her head to the side. "You *are* working on your listening. I see that. What she told me is that I could leave Sweetwater and I'd run into the same problems wherever I landed next, because people don't change. Not unless you make them." She tapped a finger to his chest.

"Like me." Brett nodded as if he knew exactly what she meant.

"Like me. Like Leanne. If we want things to be different, we have to make the change." Why was it that the hardest things to do often came wrapped in easy-to-say packages?

"So here's what I want." She moved away from him, prepared to pace as she brainstormed, but he held tightly to her hand. "I want Riley to have time to be a kid, so I'll make sure I'm here after school and when you need a break because I can do that. I want Parker to never change. I'll always love him just as he is. I want Leanne to be strong and happy, so I'll first tell her to get over her anger, and then I'll find her a job. I want Sweetwater to see you and me as a real thing, a couple with possibility, so we'll be together more often. You'll get used to it. And I want everyone to see the true me, so I'm going to show it."

Brett inhaled deeply. It had been a mouthful of words to spit out, but she had no concern how he would take them. This was the change she was going to make. She was going to trust more, protect herself less.

She might get hurt, but she might get everything she ever wanted.

"Can I make two suggestions?" Brett asked as he pressed his hands down on either side of her hips. "First, people don't like it when you tell them what to do. I have learned it's better to offer help." When she started to respond, he raised his eyebrows. "And my next…idea is this. Leanne currently has no transportation. Your car is in Sevierville. I wanted to talk to her. A car ride seemed the perfect solution. She's going to need another ride in the morning. She's expecting me at eight, but I sure have missed my kids. You could pick her up instead."

The poetic justice of his helpful suggestion was so delightful that she couldn't say no. Christina pressed a quick, hot, happy kiss against his lips and would have danced away, but he held her close enough to share a breath and deepened the kiss, his smile a sweet addition to the warm pleasure of their connection.

"No more talk about leaving Sweetwater. I can't stand it." He pressed his forehead to hers.

As her eyes drifted closed, Christina whispered, "No. This is home."

CHAPTER SEVENTEEN

WATCHING LEANNE'S FACE as the truck puttered up to the fancy hotel Brett had booked made being out so early on her day off worthwhile. Leanne was sitting on the bench outside the hotel's automatic doors, her phone in one hand as her jaw dropped.

"The last time I was in that piece of junk, we were stranded in the forest and had to walk more than a mile to the road to catch a ride. I swore then that I'd never willingly get in again." Leanne stood slowly and moved to the edge of the sidewalk, her arms crossed over her chest.

"Things change. Get in." Christina had learned that the "hurry it up" motion worked on Riley, so she repeated it. "We have to talk."

Christina hadn't been certain her bold plan would work, but Leanne yanked the door open, her lips a tight line, and slid inside. "Roll the window up. It's chilly this morning."

"You don't want to see the mess Parker made of the window. When I get my keys back, I'll return the truck and Brett will clean it. He doesn't know about it yet, and it'll be a fun surprise when he sees the gross smudges." Christina drove carefully, determined not to let anything distract them from the conversation they needed to have.

Getting it started was going to be the big challenge.

Leanne kept her head turned away, pretending to study the scenery, but she didn't complain.

In other standoffs, Christina had folded first. This time would be no different, but it wasn't going to be how Leanne expected. "Riley and Naya had a big fight and are no longer friends. As a result, Riley also has a new haircut, which you are going to love." There was no doubt in her mind about that. "Parker retains the high score in all his video games, but someday I'll give him a run for his money. Can you accept that I've fallen in love with your kids and want only *everything* for them?"

Leanne tipped her chin up. "Nothing new there. You've always loved them. I know that."

Christina nodded.

"My nagging started before Brett left town. I insisted he help me find you. Every bargaining chip I had, I used to get closer to your kids, because that's what you wanted, or to you, because I missed you. I needed you. I was worried about *you*. That is also something that never changed. Never has. Never will. You make me madder than anyone else in the world, but I have to learn to deal with it because I love you more than anyone else in this world, too. We're family. Good or bad, we stick together. You know that. How could you act like that would ever change?"

Leanne shifted in her seat. Christina tried to prepare herself because this was the sorest spot. Poking it would hurt, but they'd have to do it to heal it.

"You think I don't know how great a guy Brett is? I mean, if you can get over the perfection and his high opinion of himself, he's too special to miss. A good father. A guy who always does the right thing in this world and beats himself up over his mistakes. A good son to a difficult mother." Leanne shook her head. "Parker will have a chance to beat him someday, obviously."

As she drove through the light morning traffic, Christina tried to be patient. Leanne was working through her hurt. It would take time.

"When I left, I hated him. It's unbelievable that thirty days is all it took to ask for his help because I trusted him so much." Leanne glanced in her direction before staring out at the deserted road in front of them. "I guess I could see how easy it would be to fall for him. Thirty days changed my outlook. It could change your heart, too."

"You know I have no idea where I'm going, right? Sevierville. We're in Sevierville, but where is my car?" Would she even recognize the thing when she saw it again?

"Take a right up here." Leanne turned to scoot closer to the door, one leg folded under her as she faced Christina. "How do we make this work, Chris?"

"Small, easy steps. I'm a big believer. First, you go see your kids. Next, we make lunch and talk about everything you've learned and what you've missed, and we listen to Parker shout about hot dogs, and Riley will shock us all somehow. It seems to be her signature move lately. And then day one is over. That's it. That's all we have to do." Christina realized as she talked that she meant every word. She couldn't predict what would happen with Brett or how well Leanne would do, but she could say with some certainty that they would need to catch up and eat meals today.

"I need a place to stay. A job." Leanne sighed. "If I stay mad at you, I'm homeless."

"You aren't going to stay mad at me. It's impossible. I learned from the best how to win people over. Besides... You. Stole. My. Car." Christina turned into the parking lot where her car was parked. As she braked, she pointed obnoxiously at it. "I'm willing to let that go. You can decide to give me a chance to figure out this thing with

Brett. I mean, I'm begging you to move back in with me, to let me help you find a job. All you have to do is..." Christina inhaled. "You have to make up your mind. That's what you have to do." She propped one elbow on the door. "And bring my car back," she grumbled, "because this one has snot on the window."

Leanne jerked away from the door and slapped Christina's shoulder. "You are the worst." The giggles started as she checked her shirt and then the door, and then she couldn't do anything but laugh.

Just like that, it was all worth it.

Because Christina had no doubt that everything was going to work out. The sunshine that glinted off the windows caught in Leanne's hair and they might as well have been kids again, laughing at something else, but together.

When they finally settled down, Leanne closed her eyes. "Man, it feels good to do that."

"You have to get over this and decide to stick it out with me, Leanne. We're family. No one else would laugh like that with me." Christina cleared her throat. "I'll do my best to listen to you and we'll all go slowly, but everyone is moving forward."

Leanne nodded. "Fine. You always have been the smartest of any of us. That and the way you love makes it impossible to imagine life without you. I want the best for my kids and Brett should be happy. I think you can do that if you want to."

"I want the same things. Brett does, too." Christina rubbed her forehead. "Somehow, I've convinced myself that this dysfunctional family setup makes perfect sense."

"Let's not look at it too closely. I want to see my kids." Leanne opened the truck door. "I'll follow you home."

As she made the quick trip back to Sweetwater, Christina held those words close. *I'll follow you home.* That was where they were going.

And Leanne's reception was exactly what Christina expected and so much more. Instead of screaming his excitement, Parker was dumbfounded when Leanne walked through the door. From her spot in the living room, Christina watched him come running, freeze, and then launch himself at his mother, his arms wrapped tightly around her stomach.

"Hey, Parks, when you get quiet, I start to worry," Leanne said softly as she ruffled his messy hair.

"I missed you." He pressed his face closer to hers and Christina had to look away. Finding the people she loved and the home she wanted was one thing. Watching their dreams come true right before her eyes was too much for even a hard-hearted opportunist to withstand. Her eyes met Brett's, but she was too far away to reach him. As she started to motion to him to go get Riley, wherever she was, Parker leaned back and yelled, "Riley, get in here."

"He takes after his father," Christina muttered, and then leaned back against the wall. "Always with the orders."

"What are you yelling about?" Riley snapped as she marched down the hall. When she emerged, it was easy to see she wasn't expecting visitors. Morning hair with her short cut mainly left her looking surprised.

Or maybe she was really surprised. She froze next to her father, and then stumbled closer to Leanne. There was no angry girl left in Riley. Her words were broken, but Christina thought she said, "Mom." Then she was sobbing into Leanne's shoulder as if her heart was broken and putting it back together was painful.

Brett caught Christina's attention, and then showed her a way out, up and over the couch. He mouthed, "Privacy." And then motioned for her to hurry up.

"That's my move," Christina muttered, and took his hand to step down.

"Let's go outside. Lunch can wait." Brett led her out onto the deck. In the bright light of day, it was easier to see the wear of years of use, but the swing was still there.

"Everything okay?" he asked in a hushed voice.

"It will be. I know exactly what it will take, too." Satisfied with her morning and the future that might be if she made it happen, Christina leaned back with a sigh. "I should get one of these, a swing of my own."

"You're welcome to use mine whenever you like." Brett pulled her closer. "Or I'll find one for you. I know just the place to put it next to your cabin."

Christina turned her head to study his face. "We're going to have this same conversation a lot over the coming decades, aren't we?"

Brett frowned. "Yep. How about 'If you'd like, I can see if the old guy who made mine is still working. Then I can help you hang it. If you'd like.' Does that sound helpful without being bossy?"

Christina wrinkled her nose. "We have time to figure out where the line is."

"Yeah, we do." Brett pressed a kiss to her forehead. "Glad to have your car back?"

"Oh, you have no idea." Christina laughed to herself and stretched out next to him. "Let's stay right here for the rest of the day."

"You have the best plans," Brett said on a yawn. He stretched out next to her and the problems that had been wearing her out evaporated in the October sunshine.

This was right.

She'd made it home.

CHAPTER EIGHTEEN

Two months later

"PUT YOUR BACK into it, Brett," Leanne barked from her spot on the bed of the pickup truck Christina had nearly claimed as her own. "My new apartment is ready and I've got to set it up so I can go to work tomorrow. This is no time to take it easy."

Christina studied Brett's face and decided it was a good thing he'd put his back directly toward Leanne. Rolling his eyes at her orders would lead to more barking.

"She's really taken to this management role, hasn't she? She'll have Janet's souvenir shop under control in no time," he said mildly as he hit the cabin door with his shoulder while simultaneously turning the knob to enter.

"Like Napoleon took to France." Christina winced at the loud, wrenching squeak the door made every time someone managed to get it open or closed lately. "Or like my best friend has taken to claiming every single one of the garage sale finds we've combed this county for over the last two months. Losing my roommate was fine, but I'm going to need to find a place to sit." Janet Abernathy had been easily persuaded to give Leanne a shot at managing Sweetwater Souvenir, and it was clear that Leanne had found her calling and the mentor she'd needed her whole life. Leanne worked hard at the store, but she soaked up every bit of wisdom she could from Janet and Regina.

The first time Leanne had objected to how Christina placed her furniture, swiftly rearranging the mismatched dining table chairs into a better arrangement, had made it clear that Leanne was learning about more than running the cash register. Since she was so happy, it was difficult to be irritated.

Difficult, but not impossible.

Leanne breezed through the door on her way into the small corner of the cabin that might be called the kitchen, since it had a refrigerator and oven. "You don't mind if I pack up these, do you?"

Christina never had the chance to answer.

Without hesitation, Leanne collected the four plates and cups they'd picked up the week she'd collected her first check.

"It sounds like there's a question mark on the end, but no." Riley grinned and took the box her mother thrust into her hands. "I'm going to be a manager myself someday. I like how it works."

Parker had done little more than toss discarded newspaper in the air, and then run under it, but he was enjoying it and whatever mess he made wouldn't contribute much to her ransacked cabin.

"Should we put a stop to her naming and claiming?" Brett asked as he dropped down on the sofa. "She's not taking this, is she? I mean, not with us sitting on it she won't."

Christina plopped down beside him and draped her legs over his lap, completely worn-out from the moving that had already taken place. Janet and Regina had salvaged some pieces from Janet's latest home remodel and donated them to the apartment they were renting to Leanne as part of her compensation for managing Sweetwater Souvenir.

"The couch does not meet Janet's design standards." Christina propped her head on the arm of the couch. "It's meant for sleeping more than entertaining, and if I have to hear one more time about the perfect setup for entertaining, I will lose my…"

"Y'all, we can't be late. Regina and Janet are meeting us at the store in—" Leanne checked her phone for the umpteenth time "—thirty minutes. They're bringing the handyman who did the reno to take a look at the leaking sink and I want to get the pizza in the oven." She clapped her hands. "Moving now, cuddling later." Then she tuned on her heel, the friendly black bear that was the Sweetwater Souvenir mascot grinning broadly from her back as she marched away.

Brett squeezed Christina's leg. "You heard her. Cuddling later." He shrugged. "We could give it a try. Later."

"I need to get a swing here." As she watched Leanne carry off the lamp Christina had rescued from the side of the road, she added, "But I better nail it down."

When her eyes met Brett's, it was impossible to worry too much about replacing the things disappearing from her cabin. He also wisely did not bring up his previous offer to get her a swing.

"I like the paint." He turned his head slowly and studied the changes she and Leanne had made. "When's the next slumber party?"

They'd taken to inviting the kids over on the weekend. Pizza, loud music and enough painting to cover the White House had kept everyone busy and it was nice to watch Leanne with her children.

"The next one's at the apartment. We have permission to add summer flamingo to the walls." Christina raised her eyebrows. "Do you know how many shades of pink paint there are and how long one woman can stare at small squares before she decides? Janet may be a semipro interior designer, but I was ready to toss the paint cans in the trash before she decided."

Brett's hand on her leg was familiar and new, and no matter how long they sat there, she'd never get tired of being next to him.

"I should hire her to renovate my place."

He studied her face. "It's been a long time since it had a fresh coat of paint. If you were picking, what would you choose?"

Christina narrowed her eyes at him. "You don't change a thing there. That place is perfect."

"It's got a cramped living room and only one bathroom. There's a hole in the laundry room door from the first year Parker took karate and I've been meaning to stain the deck since I built the thing." When he smiled like he was, the corner of his mouth turned up and his eyes were so sweet, it was almost impossible not to kiss him.

"Yeah. It's perfect. A home. Don't change it." Christina bent forward. "You could put your handyman skills to work around here, though."

His eyebrows shot up and he jerked to a sitting position. "No way. You want help?"

"Help?" she repeated as if she were completely unfamiliar with the concept. "I'm not sure I understand."

He shook his head. "I get it. You don't need a knight to make your repairs for you."

Christina moved to rest her chin on his

shoulder. "But I like the way you look in a tool belt."

Brett laughed. "Have you ever seen me in a tool belt?"

"It's been too long, but I like looking at you, Officer." The smile on her lips was impossible to contain as she pressed them against his. When Brett wrapped his arms around her, nothing else mattered, not the warped wood door, her quickly emptying cabin or the next thing that was coming. Together, they could handle it.

"Fine. I'll strap on a tool belt and show off my skills." He thumped his head back against the cushion. "After my mother leaves."

Christina winced. "And Diane is coming into town...when?"

The wicked glint in his eyes was irresistible. "I don't want to give you any advance warning. I'll tell you when and where to report for dinner. We can huddle together."

"Are you two still sitting?" Leanne asked, scandal clear in her tone. "We're going to be late. My bosses are expecting us."

Brett nodded and rolled off the couch

slowly before standing and offering his hand to Christina. "You're up for dinner with Diane, aren't you?"

Leanne tipped her head to the side before the wicked grin that had always signaled trouble when they were growing up spread across her face. "Wouldn't miss dinner with Mom."

"That's what Leanne always calls her. Mom." Brett's rusty laugh got them all started.

Leanne held her hand up for a high five and Christina returned it. "I wish I'd thought of that."

"Family dinner with Riley, the punk rocker, Parker, the one with no volume control, my ex-wife and my...Christina." Brett shook his head. "She won't be back for a while. I like this plan we're putting together."

Leanne frowned at him and shook her finger. "Your Christina? You better figure out the answer to that question and soon." Then she was gone, the setting sun lighting up the small blue streak she'd added to the pixie cut she and Riley were both sporting.

"What do you think this town will say

about our family dinner? Will anyone believe it?" Brett asked as he pulled Christina to him, his eyes focused on her mouth.

"They believed we were engaged and that was nowhere near the truth." Christina leaned closer.

"Well, not yet." Brett's serious expression robbed her of breath. "But soon."

Christina could feel the weight of his stare, and she knew him well enough to predict the answer he was waiting for.

She also had enough of the old Christina left inside to want to keep him on his toes, so she smiled slowly. "Yeah. Soon."

His victory whoop rattled through the cabin and was answered by his son outside. The whole Hendrix family was wild and silly and, today, loud.

How wonderful that she'd finally found her place.

* * * * *

Don't miss the first
OTTER LAKE RANGER STATION
title from acclaimed author
Cheryl Harper:

SMOKY MOUNTAIN SWEETHEARTS

LUCKY NUMBERS *miniseries:*
THE BLUEBIRD BET
HEART'S REFUGE
KEEPING COLE'S PROMISE
A HOME COME TRUE